CAPTAIN JACK

About the Author

A charismatic, young and enthusiastic writer and author with nothing but a pen at the end of the day and a family legacy to share with people of the three P's. Pilots, Pirates and... something else beginning with P and other syllables that I will come on to later. This, dear reader, is something I wish to share with you; my tales.

As previously mentioned, I am young and enthusiastic and have a nose for a good story and, unlike a reporter, I get it right. In an... obscure way, I suppose. Anyway, don't waste your time on me; read.

Adam Hockley

CAPTAIN JACK

Vanguard Press

A CIP catalogue record for this title is
available from the British Library.

ISBN 9781784656 74-4

*Vanguard Press is an imprint of
Pegasus Elliot MacKenzie Publishers Ltd.*
www.pegasuspublishers.com

First Published in 2020

**Vanguard Press
Sheraton House Castle Park
Cambridge England**

Printed & Bound in Great Britain

Jack Evades Wolff for the Second Time!

As written by Richard Stupples in 1845
A prediction of the future from a family of embellishers.

"Dad what will life be like in sixty years?" asked little George.

"Well son, life will be, well err… life will have progressed!" Richard his father replied.

"In what way Dad?" said little George.

Richard's mind was on other things as he milked the cow. "Well," he said, "life will be… futuristic and grand!"

Little George had a good imagination, already he was brainstorming. He was only six and wanted to envisage the world as most six-year-olds do.

"Technology will be abundant," continued his father, "and everything will work with precision and the nation will grow mighty." He squeezed another drop of milk out of the cow.

He finished milking the cow and finally, his mind was on what the future would be like after fifteen minutes of being pestered by his six-year-old son.

He stood up triumphantly and carried on with his story. Although he had no facts to back it up with, he turned to the work of fiction he spun, over the lunch break alongside his inquisitive son.

"Yes," he said, "times will change drastically!"

Little George was in awe.

Although George was a dreamer, Richard knew that his son was smart and that he'd need a certain amount of facts to back up his story. At the time, there was a lot of to-ing and fro-ing of nations in overseas countries, as well as politics and various other things. So, quickly thinking Richard included this in his description.

"One day," he said, "a regime will come into power overseas that will try to dominate other countries and throw the world into war."

Little George looked at him shocked, and tears welled up in his eyes. Richard realised at that point that he might have gone a little too far. So, he backtracked slightly.

"But there will be someone, someone from England to save the day. My grandson, your son will be there," Richard said. The story was spiralling out of control. George looked at him, disappointed and confused. "He will be a Captain of a ship. Captain Jack Stupples, to be exact. And the ship will be called The New…" He had to come up with a name. He looked around him. There was a rose to his left and a piece of moss on a rock to his right. "The New Moss Rose!" he said.

George asked, "Why is the ship called The New Moss Rose? What happened to the old one?"

"Well, that burnt down," said his dad, "in an insurance scam."

"Oh, right," said George. The story was becoming interesting now. "Go on," said little George.

"Okay, Son," said Richard. "Your son, Jack Stupples, will have a crew and the world's technology will have progressed by then. So, The New Moss Rose will be able to fly and Captain Stupples will be into his alcohol, as the price will have dropped in the future!" Little George looked amazed.

Indeed, if this were a film and not a story, Christopher Nolan would be the director and Hans Zimmer would do the music. But I don't think that this story will become that big, so unfortunately you are going to have to bear with me for now, in the telling of the tale of Captain Jack Stupples and his first mate Billy Catt, or 'Moggy' as he was nicknamed aboard the ship; and their adventures on board The New Moss Rose.

Captain Jack Stupples was a not a tall man as some might have portrayed him, but just below average height in fact. I would reveal grandiose and noble things about Captain Jack, his first mate Moggy and the New Moss Rose but from the outset, the facts sounded like a big joke.

To get to the point and to avoid any confusion along the way, Jack's first mate Billy Catt was called Moggy not because his second name was Catt, you might think. No, it was because he wore paint which made him look like a cat and Captain Jack Stupples had a wind problem. Yes, sad as that may sound, it was the case. Captain Jack kept Moggy under safekeeping on board his ship the New Moss Rose, not because he was a bad sailor or anything. If anything he was a handy bloke to have around, but people fifty odd years into the future from 1845 onwards, weren't exactly too fond of people who dressed up as cats. Oh, and to make matters worse he called the paint that he wore, war paint, that made him look reminiscent of a cat; meaning that he drew whiskers on his face every morning and wore fangs, both of which he claimed were essential items needed for war. Why he wore paint that made him look like a cat no one knew.

Captain Jack only assumed he had had a traumatic experience that he had never talked about, in the war against the Germans. That wasn't uncommon, but to have someone like that aboard a ship brought its own problems. Anyway, he was a good crew member because he knew his way round the ship.

As previously mentioned, the ship, the New Moss Rose could fly. Anyway, we'll talk about that some more later on, but for now let's talk about Captain Jack Stupples.

Captain Jack Stupples lived in futuristic England, meaning that everything was powered by steam, not just the factories and the trains, but the train carriages as well and the hospitals. Even the fire brigade was steam powered, with their powered wings, carrying them high into the air to fight fires. That was futuristic England for you, and indeed most of the world were quickly catching on to the ideas of the future, and Captain Stupples was in the thick of it.

The New Moss Rose was a type of vessel called a 'Smack' and as previously mentioned, it could fly, meaning that it had a zeppelin type balloon on top, that was inflated in approximately two minutes using a can of compressed hydrogen stored in the hull. That made things easier for Captain Jack and Moggy's alcohol smuggling activities as the boat could float through the air in the clouds supposedly undetected by human eyes.

However, there was a German man who thwarted their activities. His name was Otto Von Wolff; a madman to a chronic degree with his efforts to police the skies, and he tried to foil every one of Captain Jack and Moggy's efforts to smuggle alcohol into Britain from France, to avoid tax.

Absinthe was the name of the game in the futuristic world and Captain Jack and his crew were involved with smuggling it. The Green Fairy was well sought after in Britain at around that time, and the New Moss Rose would sail happily to northern France to buy this drink. Anything further abroad was a job for the Zeppelin on top of the Smack.

Otto Von Wolff or Otto Von Pratt, as Jack called him had made enemies with Captain Jack because he 'grassed him up' for selling tax free alcohol in Ramsgate, one year before the war. Ever since, they had been enemies and Von Wolff purposely targeted Captain Jack and the New Moss Rose because, being a high-ranking German official and being laughed at in court are not things that were taken lightly by the recipient.

This all happened before the war. Essentially Otto Von Wolff the 'prat' was witness to the alcohol arriving on shore, obviously avoiding the tax warehouse before it was sold-on and as a result, Jack was taken to court. There was technically no evidence but unfortunately Otto Von Wolff managed to get hold of some. Jack, however, took the trial in his stride and made the court laugh with his antics and tales of, 'how he did it'.

Von Wolff didn't like being made a fool of. So, ever since, Von Wolff would take it on himself with his persuasive manner and ample finances, to make it as difficult as possible for Captain Jack to operate in the modern world. As a result, they were enemies.

Fortunately for Jack, he was usually one step ahead, avoiding Germany like the plague and painted the New Moss Rose a different colour now and again, so that Von Wolff couldn't detect it. Anyway, I'm spoiling the story; you get the idea, the world was futuristic from an 1840s' perspective, everything had future technology powered by steam, but just like any other era the world it had its heroes and its villains. Let's see what you Dear Reader, make of Captain Jack and the New Moss Rose.

As previously mentioned, Captain Jack lived in the future; in the Ramsgate Plains of Waterloo Street, to be exact, and we pick up the story as he takes his daily walk down to the harbour from there, as he did every morning. Jack had a sort of jolly walk; which is the best way to describe it; as he walked down the slope to the harbour, with a bounce in his stride and a smile on his face, walking down to do the job that he loved, alcohol smuggling on board his vessel.

Indeed, the Smack, the New Moss Rose was an alcohol smuggling boat that operated undercover, disguised as a fishing boat with a hidden Zeppelin stashed away on top of it. When needed, it would take a long time to untie the thing and then inflate it and release it from its platform, so it could then be filled with hydrogen.

Jack looked down the sloping road towards Ramsgate harbour. Steam emanated from sources everywhere you looked; ships, auto carriages and so on. There were even steam powered communication devices nowadays, with little puffs of *steam* to identify the people using them.

Jack observed the people who were using them. There weren't many down there at that time of the morning as it was only six o'clock. Anyway, with the amount of steam powered products being used the whole thing looked like a smog field rather than a harbour.

Jack enjoyed his morning walk down to the harbour though, it gave him a blast of fresh air to power him up, so to speak, before the daily grind began. He left his wife Maud every morning, in the house in The Plains of Waterloo Road to do various jobs around the place, while he went out to earn some money from selling alcohol. Jack loved his wife Maud just as much as his boat the New Moss Rose. In fact, the boat was like a woman to him with her perfect handling and sleek ways.

He reminisced on this as he walked down the sloping road to the harbour, leaving Maud behind, passing the fisherman's houses to his right, and the Admiralty Building to his left and towards the Smack Boys House down at the harbour. That was where Moggy came from.

Jack walked across the harbour edge to where the New Moss Rose was moored, to find Billy Catt A.K.A Moggy attending to the boat, and as usual he had his war paint and his fangs on. A group of girls walked across the harbour edge and looked at Moggy, giggling at the sight of him. Moggy stopped what he was doing on the boat and hissed at them like a cat. That was his usual response.

"Morning Moggy," said Captain Jack from the harbour's edge and he walked across the gang plank onto the boat.

Moggy looked up; he hadn't noticed him as he untied a rope. "Morninggggg Captainnn," said Moggy to the Captain.

"How is she this morning?" said Jack.

"Ssshe looksss good, Captain," said Moggy.

The Smack, the New Moss Rose was a fairly big boat, with its two massive sails and the platform on top with the deflated Zeppelin on it, which Jack told people was a spare sail. Odd; people thought, for a ship to carry a spare sail on top like that. No sailors really did that. But none the less the Smack, the New Moss Rose remained covered.

Although this was in the future, the New Moss Rose was the only ship on that side of the world that could fly, strangely enough; and Captain Stupples knew that that was what gave him his cocky persona. Catt A.K.A Moggy was only a young man and didn't have an ounce of bravado in him, which was the total opposite of Captain Jack's young at heart, happy, go lucky manner. But nonetheless, he and Moggy were good friends who sailed together on the boat.

Today's job was simple; travel to France and pick up a bit of Absinthe, sell it on British shores, tax free and no one would know the difference. All that meant was that the world had acquired better taste, in Jack's estimation. The

New Moss Rose needed five crew members in total to sail it. So that meant three more were needed.

"Where are the rest of the crew this morning, Mogg?" Jack asked Moggy.

"Nottt sssure, Captiannn," replied Moggy.

"We were supposed to leave at half six!" said Stupples. The boat the New Moss Rose included other crew members because in Jack's estimation, more hands made lighter work and also the boat needed five crew members to sail it. The trouble was to find the crew members. You see, not many sailors or craft handlers were interested in sailing a boat with a man on it who dressed like a cat and that had a big platform on top with a cotton mass on top of it, the purpose which no one could identify.

So, in essence, the men needed were people who loved to avoid tax and who loved the Green Fairy enough to grin and bear the attendant risks; but that's another story for another time, as the crew members, were dare I say it, rather reckless people. So, for now, we'll look ahead, and find out how full of clichés Captain Jack was.

No sooner were the words out of his mouth, a man popped out from around the corner of the Smack Boys House, opposite the boat's mooring, and said, "Morning Captain."

Jack looked up to see Alvin Contriteness Arkwright, a man who was unfortunately, a crew member aboard the New Moss Rose.

"Sorry I'm late Captain," said Arkwright, as he walked along, "my girlfriend has been playing up again and she wants more money off me!" Arkwright spoke as if he was talking through marbles. He was a wannabe pilot by trade but wanted to see more of the real world and of course avoid tax too; Captain Jack was a way that he could do just that.

"Morning Arkwright," said Stupples.

Arkwright looked and hesitated, "Moggy," he stated.

Moggy looked up. "Morninggg Arkwrighttt," he said.

Arkwright shuffled uncomfortably. He looked the part, meaning that he looked like a sailor who meant business with his brown ball bearing eyes and sailor's outfit. He always had a pipe cocked out of his mouth as well, but as far as usefulness went, well there wasn't much of it.

Stupples looked at him as he stood on the stern of the boat, posing. Not two minutes later out popped a fat little man from the harbour with a prominent gut and a jabbering chin and freckles. His name was Ronnie Mills. Stupples brought some things onto the boat as Mills shuffled across the gang plank and onto it.

He apologised for being late. "Sowwy I'm late, Captain," he said.

Stupples looked at him; 'a foolish guy', was the first thing that popped into his head looking at the fat, oversized man that stood in front of him. Essentially, Mills was there as fodder. He would do the menial jobs and think that he was doing a really tough job.

Stupples had met Mills in a pub in Ramsgate, and had sized him up instantly, as a waste of space. Mills wasn't a natural sailor or a crew member. In fact, he wasn't a natural anything, just a big waste of space. But Mills looked up to anything that was out of his reach or beyond him, which was a lot; physically and mentally. So, the prospect of joining a ship that could fly and a crew was like an offer of a million dollars to him. Also, to make matters worse, Mills couldn't pronounce his R's, and because he couldn't say 'irritated' and he couldn't say 'angry' because they had R's in them. He used to say it made him very 'miffed'.

Stupples knew that there was some use for this man though. All he had to do was butter him up and keep him sweet, by giving him all the menial jobs.

"Morning Mills," said Stupples.

"Yes, sowwy I'm late Captain, my Mothew was bewating me befowe I left."

Stupples didn't say anything. He was shortly followed by John Cocksure who was on his steam powered communication device as he rushed down to the harbour. All Stupples could hear from him was, "You, you, you!"

So, he naturally assumed that he was having an argument with his wife. Puffs of steam came out of the communication device as he strode along.

Cocksure arrived at the boat and finally he screamed, "Well, have it your way!" Down the communication device before grinding it to dust in his hand. The device was spread all over the harbour floor. This man was actually Stupples's cousin.

"Morning, John," said Stupples from the boat.

"Oooo morning cuz," said Cocksure to him in a friendly voice. "Morning crew." Cocksure continued, "It's a nice morning for it isn't it?"

"Morning," the rest of the crew responded.

"Meow," said Moggy.

John looked at him.

Cocksure looked at him and wondered if it wasn't for the crews strange ways and idiosyncrasies that there was no way they would put up with him. He was crazy, he was domineering, and he was violent. Any slight ripple from another crew member and they would be in big trouble with him. He got away with it though because of his large, brown, puppy dog eyes that gave him the look of an innocent person as he got on with his day to day life, but that was just a big lie. So that was the crew of the New Moss Rose in futuristic England. A desperate bunch with the capabilities of a gold fish. The only real skill came from Moggy and Captain Jack Stupples himself.

Anyway, with the sailors on board and a hull full of hydrogen and space for the Absinthe, the New Moss Rose, with its motley crew, set sail. The exact destination was Guernsey, Saint Peter Port. An odd place I know, as no one has ever really heard of it. But essentially for the Absinthe to be tax free it had to be taken from there in the first place, so Guernsey acted as a sort of middle ground for them, from where it was transported in to mainland France.

Eventually the ship set sail with the kids from The Smack Boys House watching in awe from the Harbour Arm, as the boat sailed off and out into the open sea, which was the channel across to Guernsey. The conversation was boring and dry on the way there. *When they weren't attending to the boat, Cocksure would point out every smoke trail in the sky*

22

that was left by various flying steam crafts. The craft he could identify by the steam trail left.

Everyone on board rolled their eyes as he did; with Ronnie Mills dribbling around the place and wringing his hands like a creep and Alvin's contriteness. Arkwright was posing on the deck and not really lifting a finger. Moggy was always the fastest of all the deck hands, as he was good at working the ship with her various cogs and bellows and controls that made the thing run. At that moment to conserve power and not draw any attention to the ship, they were just running off wind power, but not flying, which was fine in Captain Stupples's estimation.

He loved the wide-open spaces of the sea and harnessing the wind. It gave him a sense of wellbeing, and a thrill, and above all else, purpose, as he looked out across the waves and smelt the sea air. The ship's hull was partly made of cork, so it was a type of Q ship, which was handy when they came across a German U boat.

The channel was full of them around that time; as the war was on. Trouble was they were in a catch twenty-two situation, to a degree, as they were in danger from the water from the submarines and U boats, and also Otto Von Wolff policed the skies looking for the ship, floating through the air somewhere around France looking for Absinthe smugglers, but they had to take the risk.

The ship was pretty well armed, with its hidden on deck machine gun that popped out of the hull at the flick of a switch, the corked hull and motley crew aboard and usually no end of weaponry onboard. The fact that it looked like a normal fishing boat helped as well. Normally submarines wouldn't waste their money on ammunition to destroy a little fishing boat as it posed no danger to them.

But heaven help them if Otto Von Wolff found them for some reason, with his German private army. He owned a whole array of Subs, Zeppelins, Tanks and things, so the man was a danger and he kept showing up. The New Moss Rose had taken a battering from him before, as they tried to kill Captain Jack Stupples and Moggy. So, Captain Jack Stupples and his crew were no strangers to danger.

Eventually, without too much haste, they arrived at the island of Guernsey and sailed into Saint Peters port to pick up the Absinthe. It was a quiet little port with its maze of jetties and docks, and moored boats. Captain Jack Stupples felt proud to be trading the French booze to his own people, the British, and so his sentiments were carried along by his jovial personality as he bounded off the boat once they had moored, to meet his contact, a French twit named Jacques Morel and dare I say, there was nothing moral about him.

He was vindictive and deceitful in every way, even against his own people during the war. But there was money to be made here, so even though he had a second name like Morel that all went out the window. So, Captain Jack greeted him as he stood on the dock in the rain, waiting in his black rain coat and with a mad, Absinthe obsessed grin on his face. Moggy stayed by the boat and watched, ravelling up pieces of rope as he suspiciously watched Morel.

"Good day," said Captain Jack to the Frenchman.

"Bonjour Cap-i-tan," said Morel, in a slimy manner like the French trickster that he was.

You see any normal Frenchman would be out fighting the Germans at around that time; but not Morel and his bunch of pirates. Oh no, there was crooked money to be made here so Morel was in like a ferret up a drain pipe.

"Nice weather for it Captain isn't it?" said Stupples.

Morel looked round, "Yes it is," he said.

At that, it started to drizzle with rain. At this point the other crew members of the New Moss Rose Arkwright, Mills and Cocksure, stood on the end of the jetty, looking somewhat bewildered at Saint Peters Port, the boat and the situation, half-gagging from sea sickness.

You see they weren't natural sailors. As mentioned, they all had other occupations but the pay was better for smuggling aboard the New Moss Rose. Truthfully, they should have been out fighting a war, as after all, Alvin Contriteness Arkwright was a pilot, or so he thought. Cocksure had his uses with his mechanical mind, for building things in an up and coming industry, and Mills would be good fodder for running round, getting ammunition and other things.

But the truth was that they were all in it for the money. Well, all accept Mills for whom, as previously mentioned, sailing aboard the New Moss Rose was the opportunity of the millennium for him, and as for Moggy well, smuggling aboard the New Moss Rose was all he had ever known from boyhood.

Stupples quickly got to the point. "So Morel, we have the Absinthe? We've got to get back to England before it gets dark!"

"Ah, yes," said Morel.

At that, he clicked his fingers and two men came up beside him from inside a boat, with a big crate and put it on the jetty behind Morel. In total, there was about twenty crates to load, and eventually, after the four French pirates had loaded the crates into the boat, it was time to exchange the Absinthe for the money.

Stupples looked at Morel's grinning French face, and walked over and checked inside the crates and sure enough, there were bottles of Absinthe inside.

"So," said Morel, "you want the Absinthe in exchange for some money, right?"

Stupples nodded. "Yes," he said, "unless you were thinking of handing it over for free?"

"Well first of all," said the crook Morel. "How about you hand it over anyway, regardless whether you get the Absinthe or not!" He gritted his teeth. Stupples looked at him puzzled. "Because this is an ambush," he continued.

At that, all the boats that were around the jetty suddenly all started to raise their German flags; about five big boats in total; and Morel and his pirates started laughing wickedly.

"You have been caught Stupples!" said Morel. "By me and your good friend Mr Von Wolff!"

'Damn,' thought Stupples, 'I've been tricked.'

They loaded the crates of Absinthe onto the jetty to buy time to group themselves. Indeed, for what he assumed was some sort of ambush from the one man he didn't want to see.

'Wolff must obviously have been paying Morel off.' No sooner had the thought entered his head than Otto Von Wolff popped out on the bow on one of the big German boats on the jetty to Stupples's left.

"Guten abend Captain Stupples," stated the 'devil incarnate' to Jack, and he started to walk across the gang plank to the jetty.

Jack turned to run, but some German soldiers who had come from other boats, were already standing between him and the New Moss Rose on the jetty, their automatic rifles pointed at him, and a mean look on their faces.

Morel laughed and popped a top off one of the bottles of Absinthe and took a swig.

"You double crossing French toad," said Stupples to Morel. "How dare you!"

"Sorry Stupples," said Morel. "It's just business," and he laughed again.

You see this situation and you see a no-win situation but fortunately for Captain Jack there was always a way out. In the minute previously, Moggy had inflated the Zeppelin on top of the boat with a flick of the switch, just before giving the boat slack on the rope that tied them to the jetty, and with another flick of the switch, up popped the mounted deck gun primed ready to fire, and fire he did. Bang! Bang! Bang!

No sooner had the laugh left Morel's lips, Moggy aimed directly at the jetty stilts. He couldn't shoot the pirates on the jetty, as the bullets would pass through them and hit Jack; so the end of the jetty half- collapsed into the water with Von Wolff's German soldiers on it.

They screamed and fell into the water and Captain Jack ran and leapt off of the falling section, just in time, and jumped onto the part that hadn't fallen in and fell into Morel's arms. Morel looked shocked and Jack punched him in the face. Morel fell back onto the jetty, on his back.

Moggy aimed the machine gun at the French pirates near Jack, but just as he turned the slow-moving gun, the pirate boat drifted away from the side, in front where the jetty had been, blocking his sight. Moggy slapped his knee in frustration.

By that time, the other deck hands of the New Moss Rose, Arkwright, Mills and Cocksure had already scrambled back onto the boat at the sight of the German flags. The four other German pirates pulled pistols from their belts and aimed them at Jack, but Jack was onto them in a second, throwing himself at them, grabbing a pistol from one of them first and elbowing another in the face.

Some more German soldiers ran down and along the jetty from the other end, to try and grab Jack and to shoot at the boat in the confusion.

"Schnell! Schnell!" screamed Otto Von Wolff.

Moggy then had another idea. He powered the boat up into the air as the mass of the balloon on top had filled up with hydrogen. But it was still tied to the end of the jetty, so it lifted a piece of the jetty back out of the water, as well as sending the German soldiers flying through the air and into the water, with a splash. The balloon lifted the French pirate boat up in the air, over Jack and his ongoing battle with the French pirates and then crashed through the jetty on the other side, missing the front part that Jack was on, and blocking the other German soldiers from getting to him and the boat.

Jack had to think fast. He wanted the Absinthe, but he also wanted to stay alive and get Von Wolff. He strategised and decided in a split second that he could do all three. He managed to shoot one of the pirates in the foot. The pirate was trying to grab a gun, and pulled the trigger, firing aimlessly. He fell down and screamed and knocked another pirate into the water with a hard kick from his leg and was left struggling with the last one, locked together, as they tried to aim at one another.

"Fire! Fire!" screamed Von Wolff, cowering behind the machine gun on the bow of his boat.

The armed German soldiers stood there watching Stupples in awe. It seemed like this was the end for Captain Jack. The machine gun that Moggy had aimed at the boat from the air was at too sharp an angle so he couldn't shoot at anything and there seemed no way out.

The Union Jack that flew above the boat blew off and landed on the jetty, behind the German soldiers. Then 'crack!' The part of the jetty that the German soldiers stood on broke and they fell into the water. Von Wolff yelled and looked on in shock and misery. Jack head-butted the last French pirate who he was jostling with, and he fell into the water. At that point, he aimed the pistol at Von Wolff, who cowered away from him.

At that point Moggy knew exactly what to do. There wasn't time to bring the boat back down, so he steered it back over to where Captain Jack was. Then Cocksure, who had leaned over the side of the boat, threw the ships anchor over the side and down, with the rope attached to it. Jack grabbed onto it and swung through the air over the gap in the jetty to get to Von Wolff.

But there was another problem; Morel had grabbed onto Jack's belt and was hanging off him in mid-air. Jack struggled and he dropped the pistol into the water and then he ditched his trousers by uncoiling his belt. Morel dropped into the sea with a French wail. Jack lost his grip on the anchor rope, falling, and catching the jetties edge at the other side of the jetty.

"Damn!" yelled Cocksure from the boat thirty feet in the air.

'Okay, plan B,' thought Moggy.

He turned the boats steering wheel, so that the boat turned back again and down a little. The boats thrusters kicked in and the anchor swung and hooked underneath the other side of the jetty, snapping it loose from its stilts and pulling it up from the sea into the air with the crates of Absinthe attached. The French pirate who was shot in the foot flew off the piece of jetty and into the water.

"Aah!" he cried.

"Yay!" cheered the crew of the New Moss Rose.

"No!" screamed Von Wolff.

Morel looked up and sneered from the water. The Germans soldiers yelled. The New Moss Rose crew turned around, with a look of victory on their faces, when they realised that they were forgetting something. Captain Jack hung from the jetty, with his Union Jack under wear showing (from his loss of trousers) and Otto Von Wolff staring down at him from the jetty, with a pistol pointed at Jack's face.

He looked at Jack and in a cocky manner he said, "I'm afraid it is the end for you Stupples." He loaded the pistol in his hands. Stupples looked up at him. Von Wolff picked up the Union Jack that lay forlornly on the jetty and said, "You see this?" he said. "It's crap! Your nation will be vanquished by us!"

At that moment, something dropped down and smashed on top of Von Wolff's head, a bottle of Absinthe; judging by the smell that entered Jack's nostrils and Von Wolff passed out and fell headlong into the water, falling on top of Morel. Morel screamed.

Stupples looked up to see his cousin Cocksure standing on the piece of jetty that was hanging underneath the New Moss Rose with a bottle of Absinthe in his hand from one of the crates, cackling to himself. He had swung down from the boat to save Captain Jack.

"Come on Cuz," he said, and he threw a rope down with a noose in it. "And that's not to hang yourself on!" he said.

Captain Jack grabbed hold of the noose with his foot just as the last of the German soldiers came running down the jetty from the boats, pointing their guns at the New Moss Rose and firing. Moggy still at the controls, pushed the boats thruster control to full power, and the ship flew through the air, up and away, escaping the bullets being fired at them and Captain Jack was lifted through the air.

The Union Jack from the jetty had got hooked by the lapel, around his shoulders, and he was hoisted through the air with the flag blowing in the breeze like a cape. The crew cheered.

Morel looked up from the water and like the Absinthe swilling parasite that he was, he cried, "Look Captain Jack is a super hero!"

Shots were fired up into the air at the boat by the German soldiers on the jetty, but it was too late. The New Moss Rose was long gone.

"Till next time Von Wolff!" shouted Jack from the air.

Von Wolff looked up in dismay and cried from the water. "Curse you Jack Stupples!" His cry lasted forever.

"Yes," cackled Cocksure, "and don't you, you, you do that again!" he shouted.

Captain Jack flew underneath the boat with his cape like flag like the hero that he was, in his (union jack) underwear, with the crates of Absinthe dangling underneath the boat in his safe keeping.

Will Jack Live to Fight Another Day?

The New Moss Rose sailed back across the channel. The crew had deflated the Zeppelin and tied it on top of the Smack to avoid attention, and they were now heading back to Ramsgate, England. The trouble was that something happened on the way back. The Absinthe supply seemed to be lessening. If a bird flying across the channel could tell a story, it would be a funny one, wouldn't it? It would have seen an epic escape by a bloodthirsty German, with some tricky French pirates carrying some free Absinthe from France, to earn a lot of money. The next thing the bird would have seen would have been the New Moss Rose with a drunken crew aboard in the middle of the channel, happy to escape with their lives. Yes, the pull of the Green Fairy was too much for Captain Jack and his crew, and they sang a song with bottles of Absinthe in their hands.

"Oh! the open sea is the place for me, where the wind is strong and the cats do sing While the women who waited at home for us was always a plus." Singing was a way of life for Captain Jack and he recounted his legendary ferocity in song at sea.

Indeed, the crew of the New Moss Rose were having a knees up. After all, Captain Jack had outwitted Otto Von

Wolff again and escaped with the Absinthe from France, free of charge. In the meantime, Moggy played a steam powered fiddle complete with a steam powered speaker as they sang along; the boat just drifted along in roughly the right direction. The trouble was that all was well and good, but they forgot one crucial thing; the cargo of Absinthe was shrinking, and that was their earnings and their reward.

"Oooo isn't this lovely cuz," slurred Cocksure to his cousin Captain Jack. "We're aboard a boat. My wife's sixty miles away and we are drinking Absinthe."

Captain Jack responded by slurring, "Yes, and all thanks to our good friend Mr Von Wolff!"

The crew cheered as Moggy playfully played the fiddle, and then Captain Jack jumped up onto the steering wheel box panel and started to do impressions of Von Wolff with a bottle of Absinthe in his hand, with his Union Jack cape attached to his pants. The crew laughed again with Arkwright looking the part, with a grin on his face and a bottle in his hand, and Mills chuckling to himself as if he understood the humour; until finally Arkwright spoke up in his stupid, naïve way.

"The only trouble is Captain," he said, "now that Von Wolff knows what the New Moss Rose looks like, what's to stop him from tracking us down one day and killing us all?"

The fiddle that Moggy played went from a cheerful tune to a hoarse note and stopped. Captain Jack twitched and Cocksure glared at Arkwright.

For a while, there was a pause, all that could be heard was the splashing of the sea in the channel.

Captain Jack spoke up. "Thanks Arkwright," he said, "for spoiling our fun!"

"Well I was just saying Captain because..." Arkwright started, until Stupples interrupted.

"I know what you're saying Arkwright. Von Wolff keeps showing up and he will again," he said, "but I'm still convinced that you are spoiling our fun."

Arkwright looked at him with sorry eyes, until Jack got down from the wheel box and started pacing up and down on the deck with his hands behind his back.

"No, you are right. It is a good question," he said. "Right Mogg?"

"Righttt Captainnn," replied Moggy, his fake cats' ears blowing in the breeze.

"Yes," said Jack, "what's to stop the German swine from turning up and killing us all? With no hesitation. Anybody?" He said, "I'm open for answers." There was a pause before Mills raised his hand while Arkwright sat quietly. "Yes," said Captain Jack, "Mills?"

At that Mills said, "I don't know."

Cocksure cocked his eyes at Mills.

"Nothing," said Captain Jack. "Nothing at all is the answer! But I'm still prepared to see this venture through."

The crew went silent in agreement.

"So," Arkwright spoke up eventually, "what do we do, kill Von Wolff before he kills us?"

"Mogg?" said Captain Jack.

Moggy spoke up. "Well we'd like tto but they ssay that Von Wolff is invincibllle! And thatt he cannott be killled! We've tried manyy a time before ourselves and failed."

Arkwright pulled a naive expression then said, "What you are saying is that Von Wolff is bullet proof, or something?"

Moggy replied, "No nothingg so simple Arkwrightt", he said. "Bullet prooff would imply we acttually got a shhot at hhim. Didn't you noticce in Saint Peterss Port that he was alwways either out of rangge, or out of ssight of our sshots?"

"Almost like some other force was protecting him or is protecting him. Time and again he seems to evade our kills, knives, bombs and guns! In the meantime, he runs rampant!" The crew went silent again, and the channel flickered. "In short," said Stupples. "We need to find a way to kill him, but we don't know how to."

Essentially, after that the crew went silent and eventually they started to sing sad songs with Moggy playing on the fiddle. They carried on drinking until they were drunk, and Captain Jack fell asleep unhappy.

Later Jack awoke to find that the New Moss Rose was empty of its crew and that they weren't anywhere to be seen. It was night time and the moon shone in brilliant colours. Captain Jack looked around the boat but now no one was to be seen.

"Hello?" he said. "Anyone?"

There was no answer. In his dismay he picked up a bottle of Absinthe from one of the crates and took a sip. It tasted horrible so he threw it overboard into the sea, at that instant Jack was blown back on to the deck of the boat by what he thought was some sort of green explosion that came from the water and he looked up at the sound of a splash.

A woman came out of the sea, a pretty woman, green with wings and a frock. It was a fairy. Jack looked at the Green Fairy in shock who floated alongside the boat above the water, and glowed green in the dark.

"Greetings Stupples," said the Green Fairy. Her voice echoed and went on forever. Jack didn't say anything, but he looked at her in shock. "I bring good news," said the fairy. "There's a way, for you to survive, a way for you to kill Von Wolff!" At that, the fairy stepped onto the boat. Jack was taken aback. "Don't fear brave sailor," she said. "I am the god of Absinthe, the Green Fairy, your friend."

Jack looked at the Green Fairy, and not one to look a gift horse in the mouth he said, "How do I address you again?"

At that, the Green Fairy swished in the air a little and picked up one of the bottles of green Absinthe from one of the crates and took a sip.

"Nice," she said. Jack looked at her and then she said, "You will know when the time is right, only you will know!" Jack thought for a minute. At that the fairy said, "I have to go now my time is up."

"But wait," Jack cried as the fairy started to step back into the sea. "Why are you helping me? Do you owe me anything?"

At that the fairy said, "Let's just say Von Wolff took something from me, my body, and I believe that you can kill him and avenge me."

Jack looked at her as she sank deeper into the water.

He thought quickly and said, "Wait you said that there was a way to kill Von Wolff! How?"

"When the time is right, you'll know how. The answer is inside you Jack," she replied.

At that, she disappeared into the water and the green glow went with her. Then the bottle of Absinthe popped back out of the sea and onto the deck. Jack took it, sipped it. He woke up the next morning and he realised that it was all a dream. He looked around to see the crew asleep next to him. Arkwright, Cocksure and Mills they were all hung over, with Moggy at the steering wheel with a cold flannel on his head.

"Morninggg Captainnn," he said. "We're jusst approachingg Ramsgatte."

Stupples looked round, slightly confused. He saw Ramsgate harbour in the distance, but he was slightly perplexed by his seemingly real dream. He consulted Moggy about it while the others were still asleep.

"Mogg," he said. "I had a strange dream last night." Moggy looked at him. "A fairy who came out of the sea approached me," said Stupples, "and she told me that there was a way to kill Von Wolff."

Moggy looked at him in some dismay. "The sourcce can have that effecttt Captain," Moggy said. "We're all hungg over, ssir."

"Yes," said Stupples, "but it was so real! A Green Fairy came out of the sea and told me..."

Moggy interrupted with the best laugh that he could conjure up in the state that he was in, thinking that the Captain was joking.

"No, I'm being serious Mogg!" Jack said.

"Captainnn..." Moggy said. "The drinkk is called The Greeen Ffairy as a nickname. I'm sure you wasss just drunkk and was hallucinnating or was dehydratted or sommething and had too much to drinkkk. Afffter all you were nearly killled by Wolff. Thattt had to have some effecttt."

Jack didn't say anything more. Obviously Moggy wasn't going to listen to him, and he came to his senses quickly, realising that no one would believe him that there was a way to kill Von Wolff and that the answer was inside him. But he didn't know yet what that was. So, he kept quiet until he arrived back in Ramsgate where they all were glad to arrive that morning. They all went their separate ways after they had finally moored the boat with a struggle. Arkwright swabbed the deck before he went back to his girlfriend.

Moggy went back to, well, wherever he went to, and Captain Stupples made a quick getaway, back to his wife, Maud, while the rest went back to their stinking lives with their respective wife, mother and girlfriend.

Jack bounded joyfully up the hill, despite his hangover, to tell his wife the glorious killing that they were going to make selling tax-free Absinthe.

The first thing that Maud his wife said to him as he walked through the door was, "Jack why are you wearing the Union Jack around your shoulders?" He had forgotten he had it on.

"Ah," Stupples replied. "It is a long story My Dear."

"What do you mean we drunk it all?" Captain Jack said to Moggy in the pub the next morning after breakfast. "Why didn't you tell me?"

"Well I didn't want to breakkk the bad news to you Captainnn." Moggy cringed, "After you had that near deattth experience in Guernnsey!"

"Well why didn't someone say something to stop us from drinking it all at the time?" Jack asked.

"Welll we were all just so happyyy to get away with our livvess at the time," Moggy replied, "thatt we didn't give it a sssecond thought."

Jack put his head on the table.

"That twit Arkwright! We could have made a killing on that Absinthe selling it," Stupples said. He looked around to verify that no one listened and whispered. "Tax free I told Maud that as well!"

Moggy took a sip from his pint glass and stared thoughtfully. Then Captain Jack raised his head and looked around. In Moggy's experience Captain Jack was unpredictable, foolhardy and always pulled something out of the hat when needed. So, he waited a while.

He said, "So now we know that we drunkk all the Absintthe Captainnn, and that the ratt Morell cannot be trusteddd anymore to deal with. Where are we goinggg to get our Absintthe? He was our only Absintthe dealing contacttt. Wwhat are we goingg to do?"

Jack looked at him long and hard and then he smiled.

'There is him pulling something out of the hat,' Moggy thought.

Jack put his finger to the side of his nose and then he said, "I've got my contacts Mogg, don't worry. We'll still go to France to get it but we'll go to Brides Le Bains this time. A slightly longer journey granted, but no problem for the Zeppelin on top of the smack."

In the afternoon, they asked around whether anyone had heard reports of what Otto Von Wolff was doing or if there was word of where he was on that day. They asked sailors and fishermen around the harbour from far and wide, but no one could give them an answer, which was a shame. If they knew where he was they could build their travel plans to avoid him, as he lurked in the sky like some horror demon who waited to pounce on them at any unsuspecting moment.

Not long afterwards there were reports from some fishermen who had spotted a mine planted by the Germans in the channel not ten miles from Ramsgate. Captain Jack and his crew were quick to attend to it, trawling the mine from its ghastly, watery position and disposing of it.

"Why have you got a bullet hole in the side of the New Moss Rose?" one of the fishermen asked when they got back to the harbour. "Did you bump into some Germans?"

Jack looked and sure enough there was a bullet hole in the side of the boat, one of the shots that they had picked up in Guernsey the other day, no doubt, and they hadn't noticed it. Jack looked at Moggy and Moggy looked back.

'That twit Arkwright!' Stupples thought. 'He should have noticed it when he was tiding up!'

"Well err," he said to the fisherman, "that was one of our practice shots that went wrong ... with Moggy's gun."

The fisherman looked at Moggy.

"Meow," Moggy said.

The fisherman looked long and hard at Moggy and then concluded they just must have been idiots. One; because they must have been bad shots to practice shooting from a boat to hit the boat itself. Two; what maniac gave a gun to a man dressed as a cat. And three; what maniac dressed up as a cat in his day to day life?

Anyway, eventually a few days later after some rest it was time to plan their next trip to France, as their money had slowly dwindled.

All five crew members stood at Captain Jack's living room table looking at a map of France, all the way from the English Channel down to the Mediterranean Sea. It was a good map, the same map that they used every time for their various rendezvous in France, where they met the creep Jacques Morel to trade money for Absinthe.

The map had had its uses; its good fortune and its bad fortune at sea and in the air, but nonetheless it was still just a map and Jack knew it. It wasn't going to stop them from dying. They gazed at it, while Mills dribbled over it. The trip from Ramsgate to Brides Les Bains was long, even by air. Captain Jack thought, staring at it,

"In light of recent events," he said. "I have decided not to go to Brides Les Bains to meet my back up Absinthe contact, but to look elsewhere, instead." He took the map and screwed it up in his hands. The crew looked on in shock. "I'm afraid France is a big no, no, with Von Wolff lurking round it, looking for us so that he can kill me. This job is even too much for the New Moss Rose. I declare this meeting closed. Thank you and goodnight."

He started to walk away when suddenly a green woman popped out of nowhere and the next thing, she down on the chair near him and it wasn't his wife. She was beautiful and she glowed green like a fairy.

"Greetings Stupples," said the Green Fairy.

Jack was taken aback again. "Evening," he said.

The fairy swooped up right next to Stupples and said to him. "Why fear Von Wolff? Go to Brides Les Bains to find your Absinthe contact."

In the meantime, all the crew saw was Stupples stopping short, on his way to the door as if he were paralysed.

"Captainnn," said Moggy from the table.

"Von Wolff is powerful and influential." The fairy continued, "Yet he is weak."

"I fear that Von Wolff will kill us," Stupples said.

"Do not fear Von Wolff, Stupples," she said. "I will protect you. You'll see."

With that, she disappeared into a green haze as she cried out the words, "Go to Brides Le Bain, Stupples." Then there was nothing.

Captain Jack turned around to see the crew looking at him from the table. He coughed and went pale.

"Arre you okay, Captainnn?" Moggy asked.

Stupples thought about telling them about his daydream, but he knew that they'd never believe him. If you were in Jack's situation yourself and saw a vision of a beautiful green woman who told you to go on a suicide mission your normal reaction would be to say no; but fortunately for Jack, well he just couldn't resist.

With his 'devil may care' attitude, his good will and his happy-go-lucky demeanour, he said, "We will go to Brides Les Bains!"

The next morning the crew and the boat were all ship shape and ready to sail to Brides Les Bains in France. The cork lining of the hull had been checked and the hydrogen canister had been refilled.

Moggy pottered along on the boat, neatening up supplies and double-checking rations for the journey, while the others made themselves useful.

"All set Mogg?" Captain Stupples asked.

"Aye, aye Captain," Moggy replied.

The boat then set sail with their women all standing at the harbours edge, waving them off. Maud, Jack's wife sobbed away into a handkerchief with the other women. You see they'd travelled this far before but not very often, so this was a big trip in the minds of some, like Mills.

For a minute, Jack thought that he saw a green woman standing at the dock, but then he realised that it must have been his imagination. The only other person who knew that the New Moss Rose could fly, other than Jack and the crew was Maud, Jacks wife. The crew was sworn to secrecy otherwise they would be in big trouble with Cocksure. Cocksure was had been involved in the building of the New Moss Rose. Okay, he wasn't the designer or the architect or the brains behind it, but his little bits of engineering skills came in handy with the workings of it.

Granted they were usually the bits that packed up quickest on the boat, but nonetheless, the parts that he was involved in designing came in handy very often on their voyages.

Moggy helped to build the boat, but he seemed to have more of a knack for steering it than Cocksure.

"Why were the women crying Captain?" Moggy asked Jack as they sailed out of the harbour, incognito. "We'll only be gone for five days maximum."

"Well," Jack replied. "It is a combination of things Mogg. Women are complex and there is danger and difficulty on our journey."

Moggy looked blank. He was naive when it came to women.

"Oh," he said.

Although the New Moss Rose could fly and was a good craft, as a rule it needed frequent servicing of its steam powered engine to keep it running.

Every day it needed servicing and that would prolong their journeys. That being said, it was hard to find locations to do that in France as no one on that side of the world had seen a flying boat before. For that reason, they had to be covert regarding the boat, and they had to find someone who could service it and keep their mouth shut. The problem with travelling far on the New Moss Rose was that the ship was fast in a quick burst but it would then use up all its energy, whereas Captain Jack planned to conserve power and to take a slow trip down to Brides Les Bains, so forty miles an hour was the name of the game.

Jack had marked a point on the map of France where they would have their servicing done by another French trickster named Claud Boyer, who was drunk silly half the time with Absinthe. All that was needed to keep him quiet regarding the New Moss Rose though, was a bit of Absinthe; simple really. Although Jack did make it seem that way. The place they needed to stop to re-service the engine of the New Moss Rose was in Chaumont, about half way in France and fortunately in Brides Les Bains itself. So once the New Moss Rose crossed about half way across the channel Moggy turned on the Zeppelin mode. Two minutes later it rose into the air and then he pushed the thruster lever to about forty miles an hour and the boat moved gracefully in the air, through the clouds.

The journey that day was long and boring, with little conversation between the crew members and even less "Meows" from Moggy. Essentially, although they had a compass on the boat to point them south they would bring the New Moss Rose down every now and again below cloud level, so that they could see the ground to confirm that they headed in the right direction, and to get a more accurate bearing of where they were. The boat hung grandly, with the Zeppelin on top. Stupples looked up in admiration. Birds passed them, flying through the sky, as Moggy looked up at them.

Although the journey was long fortunately the weather was good and still.

'It is almost as if some magic fairy was in control of the weather,' Jack thought.

After seven hours of floating silently, they arrived at Chaumont. They brought the boat down on the outskirts of the town, where anyone from a distance would just assume it was some sort of Zeppelin. They had been shot at before by French people who thought that it was a German Zeppelin, so they had to be careful. Their contact Boyer stood triumphantly on the green earth as the New Moss Rose gracefully floated down from the sky, towards him.

"Bonsoir!" Boyer shouted to Stupples from the ground.

"Bonsoir!" Stupples shouted back at him, from the Zeppelin and he jumped off of it before it landed gently with a creak on the grass.

"She looks good Cap-it-an," said Boyer.

Stupples looked up at her.

"Yes she does," he said.

Boyer would also put the crew up for the evening at his farm house, while he worked on the New Moss Rose overnight, all in exchange for Absinthe. His wife gave them all food in his farm house, while Boyer moved the New Moss Rose into his industrial sized warehouse, to work on it. He serviced the steam engine and re-filled the hydrogen canister in the hull. Not much was said between the crew and his wife, they just ate and had a few drinks before going to bed.

The next morning, they were primed and ready to go. The trouble was; if they had known what lay ahead of them they would have turned back that morning, no matter how many different coloured fairies came to them and told them that it was going to be all right.

The hints were there though, like for instance, about three and a half hours into their journey to Brides Les

Bains, a massive Zeppelin carrying a German flag came out of nowhere through a cloud to the east.

"Whoa!" Moggy cried from the steering wheel as the German Zeppelin headed towards them, but it was too late.

Moggy turned the steering wheel, but the German Zeppelin had crashed right into the side of them. A grinding noise sounded as the balloon on top of the New Moss Rose crashed into the German zeppelin. Stupples looked up to see Otto Von Wolff's face pressed against the screen of the cabin, underneath the Zeppelin, with a look of shocked anguish on his face, knowing that he had missed the chance to shoot them down, even though he was right next to them.

Obviously, it was a massive coincidence that the two air ships had bumped into one another like that. But it was too late. They passed one another and then disappeared into the clouds away from one another, before anyone had a chance to do anything.

The crew of the New Moss Rose looked at one another silently, in shock at their near miss with Von Wolff. Moggy, as a reflex action put the thrusters on full to give them some distance.

Fifteen minutes later when they had made a bit of ground at a fast pace, Moggy turned the thrusters down to save power and after ten minutes of silence arguments erupted between the crew members of the New Moss Rose about their close call with Von Wolff. They all believed that it was one another's fault; from some of their perspectives it was Captain Jack's idea that had put them into enemy territory, from others it was Moggy's fault as he was driving. Some thought it was because of Cocksure's ignorance. The general consensus was that the blame lay with Arkwright and Mills for being bad lookouts as after all,that was their job. Captain Stupples kept a cool head and he made them both swab the deck as punishment.

A few hours later they arrived at Brides Le Bains and met their second contact just behind one of the mountains, to keep the New Moss Rose a secret from the main town. A small argument erupted about their near miss with Von Wolff but it was all put back in place by Captain Jack.

Twenty minutes later, after a call was made on Cocksure's steam powered communication device, another of Jacks contacts came down the road to where the New Moss Rose had perched on a rock after they had packed the zeppelin away; on a steam powered carriage to pick them up. To anyone passing it would have just looked like a boat on the mountain, which would have looked a bit strange granted, but no one really went to that side of the mountain anyway, or that high, so it was safe.

The contact who picked them up was another Frenchman with another French sounding name that Jack had forgotten, but nonetheless, he picked up the crew of the New Moss Rose, and took them to their lodgings, in the centre of Brides Le Bains. From there it was supposed to be an easy ride, meaning that Jack and his crew would go to sleep and then spend the next day loading the New Moss Rose with Absinthe and would service it at Chaumont, and then go back home. Luckily, Jack had his contacts to do all this eh?

They stayed in a humble tavern that night and didn't drink or really talk, and they barely ate due the state of their nerves, after their near miss with Von Wolff and his Zeppelin.

The next day they all woke fairly early to a bright day and they wasted no time in getting down to the Absinthe warehouse to help load the Absinthe merchandise onto the boat. A gaggle of three steam powered auto carriages, with trailers waited outside the warehouse just down the road from the tavern with three dodgy, Alpine looking men and one woman loading small Absinthe crates onto the trailers and into the auto carriages.

The leader of the four who had picked them up the previous day, who Jack remembered was named Baptiste Lenoir, approached them as they walked up to the warehouse.

"Sorry we'll have to take multiple trips to the New Moss Rose as I could only find four trustworthy people for the job. It will take longer to load. One of them is my wife," he said, gesturing to the female helping with the crates of Absinthe. "She is trustworthy," he said. "I could only get hold of four auto carriages, so we'll have to make more trips."

"That's fine," Jack said. "Let's just get it loaded up!"

They did so, and with the four Alpine tricksters and the crew of the New Moss Rose, it was loaded up quickly but the trouble was the distance between Brides Le Bains and where the New Moss Rose was, up the mountain and behind it. Granted, there was a road there, but it was still a long drive. However, drive it they did and, on each trip, they loaded-up the hull of the New Moss Rose, with the crates of Absinthe.

Jack kept an eye on the sky as he travelled back and forth in the auto carriage up and down the mountain. He had a suspicion that Von Wolff would appear, so, he and the crew kept their pistols tucked firmly in their belts; but then again, he had been wrong before. He was hell bent on getting the job done as quickly as possible.

It took the best part of the day to finish the job of loading the Absinthe onto the New Moss Rose and to get his other mechanical contact to do a remote service on the steam powered boat which also took a while. It was always amazing to see how criminals seemed to work more efficiently, do a better job and complain less than non-criminals. But after a long day of hard work it was back to the tavern, with the crew of the New Moss Rose and the four Alpine crooks who had helped them to load the Absinthe, for a drink; except for the mechanic who worked overtime, late into the night on the New Moss Rose and the first mate Moggy who stood there with a torch and an automatic rifle, guarding the New Moss Rose with his life out of choice. He was prepared to stand there all night if needs be.

Meanwhile, in the tavern, the other crew members of the New Moss Rose sat there laughing with the four Alpine crooks about their day and the killing that they had all made or were going to make with the Absinthe and laughing about their love of the sauce the 'Green Fairy'.

One person was silent though; Captain Jack. Slowly, but not reluctantly, he gave them the Francs that he owed the four Alpine crooks for the Absinthe, but that was nowhere near the killing in pounds that they were going to make back home in England. The four Alpine crooks laughed in awe at the money and Lenoir took it on behalf of his team. He twiddled his French moustache and twitched.

"Very Good Captain," he said. "I hope that our partnership will carry on for many, many years." At that, he laughed.

Lenoir and the rest of the crew of the New Moss Rose cheered, and Jack sat silently, with his head lowered. Lenoir lit a cigar and looked at him, puzzled.

Captain Jack finally spoke up. "Actually," he said, "I'm not that happy with what I had to do." Lenoir made a puzzled sound. "It's just that I'm sick of dealing with scumbags and risking my life when I have a wife at home and a good pleasure boat to love." With that, Jack got up from the table. Lenoir looked challengingly at him. "I'm going to check on Moggy and the New Moss Rose," Jack said, as he walked out.

Lenoir got the picture, and responded "Hey," to the insult of being called a scumbag.

He began to stand up, but then, Cocksure spoke up, and said aggressively, "Leave him Lenoir. We think he's had enough of all of this."

Lenoir did what he was told, and he sat down, even though it was four against one. It was funny the controlling effect that Cocksure had on people, even when he was majorly outnumbered. Cocksure continued, "We think that he's had enough of Absinthe, Zeppelins and Von Wolff!"

"Ah," said Lenoir. "I've heard about that. Wherever Captain Jack goes, Von Wolff turns up to try to foil his plans."

"Yes, that's right," Cocksure replied.

Captain Jack walked through the quiet ancient streets of Brides Le Bains with its old Alpine farm buildings and houses that lined the streets. Not many people were around at that time of night. They were all tucked away in the taverns or in the bars or eating charcuterie.

What Captain Jack didn't know though was that in the darkness, he was being followed by three black trench coats who didn't mean well. The problem was that they weren't just brawling pirates or the local scumbag thugs. These were expert German assassins; agents of Von Wolff no doubt, and Captain Jack had no idea that they were following him as he staggered through the town, drunk, making his way up towards the New Moss Rose to check on Moggy.

Jack had just turned down a dark alley that led to the main road up the mountain, when the three assassins pounced on him. Two came from ahead of him and one from behind. Jack barely saw them. Before he knew it, he was pressed against the cobbled wall of a farm building by two men, with a knife held at his throat, by the other. Jack screeched.

"Captain Stupples, on behalf of Otto Von Wolff, tell me the location of the New Moss Rose or you'll die," said an insidious sounding German voice from under his hat. Jack struggled, but it was useless. The three German agents were big and strong, and they held him in place.

The German gritted his teeth. "Where is the New Moss Rose?" he barked.

"I don't know," Captain Jack replied.

They threw Jack against the opposite wall, just in time for Jack to pull out the pistol that he had stashed in his belt. He turned, but the German agent was fast and he knocked it, upsetting his aim. The pistol went off and by a stroke of luck, the bullet must have hit something metal on the wall opposite in the alley, as it ricocheted back from whatever it had hit, probably a metal brace; and then it bounced back, and blew the German agent's head off. The pistol had disappeared into the darkness down the alley.

Captain Jack acted fast. His life and his love of Maud drove him on. So he grabbed the knife off the falling body of the dead German agent and drove it into the chest of the second. He screamed but before the third German agent could pull out a knife, and drove it towards Jack he moved out the way and it hit the wall. Jack had to drop the knife to move as quickly as he did, the last assassin with with lightning reflexes had swiped the blade round to his right. Jack anticipated the move and dropped his blade to give himself free hands to cartwheel backwards, and spring back upwards, dodging the agent's blade.

The only trouble was that there was a big marauding German with a knife coming towards him, and Jack was weapon less. Jack backed off, walking backwards with his hands behind him. If what he anticipated was going to happen, he had to act fast.

The German agent laughed and said, "Now you die" He laughed again. He threw the knife at Jack. It soared through the air, spinning like a death blade before Jack caught it by the hilt by holding his hand in front of him he quickly threw it back at the German as hard as he could. It plunged into the German's head and he fell back, dead. Jack paused for a minute. He hesitated in disbelief at the lack of time that they had, but he had to think fast to save himself and the crew. Brides Le Bains wasn't a safe place to be anymore. Von Wolff knew that they were there.

He sprinted as fast as his legs could carry him to where Lenoir had parked his steam powered auto carriage, just South of Brides Le Bains. He had swiped the key off his old French mate, previously without him even knowing, he jumped in and accelerated as fast as he could up and around the mountain towards the New Moss Rose.

The night was clear with a few clouds in the sky, and the headlights lit up the mountain road in front of the auto carriage. Eventually he reached the New Moss Rose, perched on the rock, and as luck would have it; the mechanic had finished servicing the craft and Moggy was standing next to the craft, talking to him in the dark. Moggy at the sight of the auto carriage knew that something was up.

"Moggy!" Jack cried, flinging himself out of the auto carriage and sprinting towards the New Moss Rose at full pace. "Open the hydrogen canister!"

Moggy knew that something was up and that they needed to pick the other crew members up because of the danger. So, he did as he was ordered, and he immediately jumped into the boat and flicked the switch. The Zeppelin Smack began to rise fast, and minutes later, the balloon began to float in the air and with the thrusters on full, Moggy and Jack began to make their way back around the mountain to Brides Le Bains.

Fifteen minutes later, the rest of the crew of the New Moss Rose made their way out of the tavern into the night, cackling in their success as they did. Who knows what they were doing, but just as they made their way outside, they were ambushed by a gang of German master assassins wearing trench coats and black hats. Cocksure, Arkwright and Mills all screamed but a guardian angel watched over them.

The New Moss Rose floated silently above the tavern in Brides Le Bains with Captain Jack at the wheel and Moggy with a long-range rifle, leaning over the side of the boat with the gun pointed at the German assassins. He was a crack shot. Crack, crack, crack, crack, crack Moggy's gun sounded and all five German assassins fell down dead at the feet of Cocksure, Arkwright and Mills, with a bullet in each of their heads.

"Come on chaps," Captain Jack said over the side of the New Moss Rose "We leave for England now!"

With that, Moggy threw a rope ladder over the side and the three crew members clambered up into the craft. A gaggle of local French people came out of the tavern and the houses at the sound of the gunshots in time to see the New Moss Rose fly away into the night.

The time was one a.m., but in Captain Jack's mind there was no time like the present and Von Wolff was near, Jack could sense it. The trouble was that there seemed to be an unnaturally strong wind coming from the west, so they had to hang in the air and anchor themselves to a rock. Moggy abseiled down a rope and attached the boat to the rock, ten miles northwest of Brides Le Bains for the next twelve hours until the next day. The wind died down a little, but the trouble was that twelve hours later Mills had spotted something in the morning light that the devil himself could not have imagined.

Five of what looked like armed Zeppelins approached them flying from the east in the direction of Germany was where the zeppelins came from. The Germans had invented Zeppelins and the world was at war with them, so even Mills worked out that it wasn't a good thing. Mills looked round and screamed silently in fear, and the other crew members looked at him. Captain Stupples lay there with his hat over his eyes resting. Mills tried to scream again but it was useless. He was such a buffoon it was unbelievable.

Captain Jack heard him. "What is it Mills?" he mumbled from underneath his hat. "The magic tooth fairy is coming, is she?"

"No!" Mills screamed. "Wowse!"

At that moment, Jack jumped up and he looked with the rest of the crew members towards the east and saw the five Zeppelins approaching. Stupples knew that it was Von Wolff.

"Damn!" he screamed. "Mogg, cut us loose! Head south west with the wind."

Moggy cut the anchor loose with a knife and the New Moss Rose drifted with the wind in a south westerly direction. Moggy jumped onto the controls and put the thrusters onto full. Stupples kept his eyes fixed on the German Zeppelins coming from the north east.

"Men to arms!" he cried out.

The other four crew members, including Captain Jack went into the hull and grabbed long range rifles. They crouched at the back of the boat and aimed at the German Zeppelins who were out of range at that moment but who were sure to catch up soon.

In Captain Jack Stupples mind this was it! All faced their deaths, but he kept quiet. It was a no-win situation, he could sense it. The wind was strong and it blew them the wrong way, away from England and they were outnumbered. In their journey towards the Mediterranean Sea, the Zeppelins came closer and closer; so close in fact that that they were within shooting range.

"Fire!" Stupples cried. They took pot shots at the Zeppelins from the New Moss Rose with minimal effect. "Don't skimp on bullets lads!" Jack cried.

Cocksure even jumped onto the deck grabbed the machine gun and fired but it had no effect, because the Zeppelin balloons even with holes in them still could float. The Zeppelins fired back. Moggy counted a few bullet holes above in the cotton mass of the Zeppelin.

"We're going to lose power!" Stupples cried. "Shoot them. Bring them down!"

It was no good though. Four hours later, somewhere over the Mediterranean Sea, they ran out of power and they had run out of bullets as well. The boat stopped, and it hung in the air over the sea.

"Crap!" Stupples cried. "Moggy bring us down. We'll stand more of a chance on the water. Up here we're sitting ducks."

Moggy turned, hissed at the German Zeppelins and then deflated the New Moss Rose's Zeppelin by lifting a lever and they slowly fell down through the air towards the sea, bottom first. Although it seemed like a slow descent the boat crashed into the sea quite hard, sending all the crew members face first onto the deck. Moggy smashed his face on the deck in the confusion and his forehead started to bleed.

"Now point us towards Spain Moggy!" Jack cried. "We'll be protected there. They are not in the war."

Moggy did what he asked. He engaged the propellers and at full pace, they sped through the waves. It was seven p.m. and a storm had started. The waves were big and black and they crashed against the side of the boat. Thunder and lightning crashed down from the sky, lighting up the sea and the New Moss Rose in the water. It was an unusually angry storm. The benefit that came with it was that the storm had deterred the Zeppelins, plus it was dark, so they had turned back. The crew cheered.

"Shall I slow down Captain?" Moggy asked.

"No full speed ahead!" Jack cried. "The quicker we get to Spain the better."

The trouble though is that fate can be an evil thing. Twenty minutes after heading towards Spain through the storm tossed waves, a massive surge of sea water rose up in front of the New Moss Rose as it sped along.

"What the hell is that?" Jack cried out.

"I'm not sure Captain," Moggy replied. "Some sort of eddy."

At that moment, a massive submarine emerged from the depths of the Mediterranean right in front of them. The tower rose first, and then the rest of it. It looked black and menacing; half floating in the water. The crew of the New Moss Rose looked at it in disbelief, but before anyone could do anything the boat had crashed head long into the sub, bow first, and it rose up a little at the front and then stopped.

The waves and the storm continued. Jacked looked in disbelief at the submarine. Then a hatch opened on the sub in response to the collision.

The devil incarnate himself popped out and cried out over the crashing of the waves. "Good evening Captain Stupples!"

A lightning bolt flashed and thunder crashed. Jack looked in absolute fear and anguish at the face of Otto Von Wolff. Black waves crashed over the New Moss Rose, soaking the crew.

As a reflex Jack cried out, "Port!"

With the propellers still spinning Moggy swung the steering wheel to turn the ship to port, and knocked the sub sideways knocking Von Wolff over onto the edge of the submarine's hatch. He cried out.

The New Moss Rose sped southwards through the waves and the sub trailed them. Lighting crashed. Every now and again, Moggy looked to see the odd torpedo speeding through the waves next to the boat. Fortunately, boats, are generally faster than submarines. That was where Von Wolff showed himself as a bit of an idiot. Shots were fired from the submarine's on deck machine gun, hitting the New Moss Rose.

Moggy steered the boat in an evasive course, to evade the shots and the torpedoes; until one fatal torpedo just missed the back of the New Moss Rose but blew the propellers off. Water flew up in the air behind the boat and the New Moss Rose suddenly stopped dead in the waves.

"Blast!" Stupples cried. They were now sitting ducks. The submarine approached half in and half out of the water. "Damn!" Stupples cried out. "I've doomed us all! We're all dead!" Cocksure, Arkwright and Mills screamed.

At that moment, as if in reply, a massive wave washed up against the other side of the boat and it knocked Jack over board and into the sea. Black waves crashed over him and were lit by a lightning flash. Jack looked up through the water as he sank to see the silhouette of the New Moss Rose rocking backwards and forwards above him. This was definitely it, Jack was sure of it, his death and the crew's death. The Absinthe was going to a watery grave amid the destruction of the New Moss Rose. Von Wolff had won.

Stupples slowly sank deeper and deeper; with the current and the waves that pulled him down. He didn't struggle, this was the end.

Suddenly, out of nowhere, a faint green glow came up from the depths below him, and it grew stronger and stronger rising upwards towards him. Jack watched the green light as it gradually changed, becoming brighter. The

Green Fairy rose up next to him out of nowhere. Jack looked through the water, in surprise.

The fairy said, "Don't give up Jack, remember only you know how to kill Von Wolff. Jack the answer is inside you!"

Jack screamed through the water. "I don't know how and now we're all going to die!" Bubbles erupted from his mouth. The Green Fairy shook her head and then she disappeared with a green glow. "No wait!" Stupples screamed through the water using the last of his breath. "Don't go!"

The fairy disappeared and with all the breath leaving him, Jack saw the silhouette of a fish beneath him coming up from the depths and it got bigger and bigger as it came up, and as it got bigger and bigger, Jack identified it as not being a fish but a whale. Jack was a sailor and not naive when it came to sea creatures, so he had realised that it was not a fish, but a massive Sperm whale. It came up and swam right next to him as Jack continued to sink, but something happened as the whale swam up towards the surface Jacks coat got caught on the whale's fin and it pulled him up and up.

Maybe it wasn't his death, after all? Before he knew it, the whale suddenly turned and flung Jack up through the water, up to the surface. He started to black out from lack of oxygen when a strong hand grabbed him just beneath the surface and pulled him up and out onto the deck of the New Moss Rose. Jack looked up. It was Moggy, hanging off the edge of the boat. He saw Jack and pulled him out of the water.

The storm continued to rage as Stupples gasped for air on the deck of the New Moss Rose. He looked to see Otto Von Wolff's submarine, coming through the waves, with the deck gun primed and ready to fire at them and the face of Otto Von Wolff and a few German soldiers on the outside of the sub all looking and laughing.

"I'm afraid Stupples, that this is the end for you, yet again!" Von Wolff cried out. He and his soldiers continued to laugh.

'The Green Fairy lied,' thought Jack, and he closed his eyes ready to feel a bullet in his gut.

At that moment, a massive bolt of lightning crashed down onto Von Wolff's sub, and it shattered the deck mounted machine gun and set it on fire. Von Wolff screamed and fell over. The lightning had also taken out a few of his soldiers in the process.

The crew of the New Moss Rose cheered and to improve matters even more, a massive wave came up, and carried the damaged New Moss Rose away from the burning sub, like a triumphant hero. The wave rolled on unnaturally, leaving Von Wolff and his sub behind. Another bolt of lightning had struck the back of the sub and had shattered the propellers. All Von Wolff could do was look on as the New Moss Rose sailed happily away, while his sub was crippled and on fire, all caused by a bolt of lightning.

Shortly after that, the storm died down and the wind became strong but sailable and it turned into a westerly in the night. Jack ordered the sails to be lowered. The crew did what he ordered and the New Moss Rose sailed happily towards Southern Spain, through the night.

A few days later the propellers were repaired as best they could be in Andalusia, and a service was done on the steam engine by some local Spanish mechanics, in return for some Absinthe. The hydrogen canister was refilled. The cotton Zeppelin on top of the Smack was in pretty good condition with just a few holes here and there, but still quite useable. Rations were also given to them as the Spanish knew that they were English. What they did afterwards was to fly over Spain to the west of France and then they sailed the rest of the way back to Ramsgate, as they didn't have enough power to carry them all the way to Chaumont, from the south of Spain. Captain Jack Stupples and the crew of the New Moss Rose lived to fight another day.

The Fairy's Final Gambit

"Get your tax-free Absinthe!" Captain Jack Stupples shouted at the edge of the harbour in Ramsgate where the New Moss Rose had been moored, two weeks after the last escapade.

A gaggle of interested people emerged in front of Jack and the crowd grew bigger and bigger, listening to Jacks antics of how he had obtained the Absinthe from France. He told his tale of the chase through the Mediterranean Sea and his close call where he nearly drowned and how a Sperm whale had rescued him. This was Jack's way of celebrating his success, boasting, telling his tale of 'how he did it,' and making money in the process; genius really! Besides, the Absinthe had literally gone through hell and high water to get to where it was now in Ramsgate stored in the hull of the New Moss Rose, so it was worth the tale. The trouble was that although it was a good tale, the people who listened in awe still thought that he was making it up.

Retired men and woman, fishermen, children, criminals and shipbuilders all stood around who were interested in the story and they became interested in the Absinthe because of the story. The Absinthe sold pretty easily and what they didn't sell in bulk, stragglers like the people in the crowd who listened at the time would buy it. Something had changed though.

"What do you mean a sub popped out of the Mediterranean?" one of the people in the crowd asked. "How did Von Wolff know where you were going so he could land exactly there in his submarine?"

"Well…" said Stupples, actually he hadn't thought about that.

It was a valid point, so no wonder people didn't believe him. It was far-fetched that Von Wolff's sub knew exactly where the New Moss Rose was going to drop out of the sky into the sea and then met them there. The trouble was that Jack gave away the New Moss Rose's secret which he didn't care about, after his second near death experience at the hands of Von Wolff. Again, it was almost as if some other force had protected or had guided them both, him and Wolff.

Stupples spun a good yarn.

"Well," he continued, "you have heard of this concept of steam powered radar, haven't you?" The crowd looked at one another.

"Well, yes," they all said in agreement.

"Well," said Stupples again, "the Germans have adopted it now and are using it against me!"

The crowd went silent. Stupples looked angry.

One bloke from the crowd spoke up. "No, sorry Stupples," he said. "We'll buy your Absinthe, but we don't believe you regarding your story, sorry."

Moggy, who was on the deck of the New Moss Rose grabbing bottles of Absinthe out of the hull for people buying it, slapped his forehead in a daft moment. Stupples watched.

The crowd in front of the New Moss Rose began to murmur and shout. "We just want the Absinthe Stupples, not your ridiculous story, flying boats and things, cor!"

It could have been worse, he supposed. His story could have put them off buying the Absinthe all together; so again he didn't look a gift horse in the mouth and he just accepted the sales that they made. The people in England had heard of Von Wolff, but the trouble was everyone who were not on the German's side wanted to kill him and as far as they were concerned, Stupples's tale was just a tall yarn. No, with regard to Von Wolff, Stupples was on his own. Random individuals from the crowd came out and started to buy the Absinthe off Jack though, and they were making a killing on it.

At that moment, the Home Guard Brigade marched down the harbour edge just below the road that went up to the town, with the Captain marching in front of them chanting, "Left, right, left, right." It was a fairly big brigade and they were all dressed as soldiers, but they were really all has-beens and bums. They came down to the harbours edge and again random Home Guard soldiers fell out from the brigade and started to buy the Absinthe off Stupples and Moggy.

"Morning Captain Smith," Stupples said to the Captain of the Home Guard Brigade as he watched him selling the Absinthe.

"Morning Stupples," said Captain Smith. "Nice morning for selling Captain."

"Indeed," said Stupples. "Indeed it is."

Captain Smith looked around at the remaining bottles of green Absinthe.

"Morning Moggy," said Captain Smith as Moggy brought another small crate of Absinthe out of the hull.

"Morningggg Smmith," Moggy replied.

"Making another killing on Absinthe I see Stupples," said Smith.

Stupples smiled. "Always!" he said.

Captain Smith was an old boy who had his hay day in the army in the eighteen eighties; he was a bit stupid now and again but he had good usage as far as the Home Guard was concerned. The lads from the Home Guard Brigade brought their Absinthe.

"Thank you," Stupples said to them.

"I hope your men enjoy their sauce," Stupples said to Captain Smith.

"They will do, they will do," said Smith. His men fell back into line with a couple of bottles each in their bags. Smith shouted. "Right lads back to the depot." At that, he turned around and they marched off with their Absinthe, back down towards the harbour with Captain Smith chanting, "Left, right, left, right."

The crowds were there just to buy some Absinthe. Stupples looked at Moggy and half smiled at the situation. Eventually the crowds died down after they had purchased their Absinthe.

Next, it was down to the local pub for a late lunch.. Rations were the name of the game and a pint. The other three crew members of the New Moss Rose, Cocksure, Arkwright and Mills sat with them for lunch and to get their pay. Mills got the least pay, as the journeys that they took on the New Moss Rose to get the Absinthe were partly to educate for him. Moggy dealt with the money and he handed the cash to them over the bar table, while Stupples boasted about their latest success with Von Wolff and the killing that he had made on the Absinthe. There were only two small crates left, which was good after just a morning of selling. They all cheered.

"Hurray for Captain Jack Stupples," they all chanted. "Hurray for the death of Von Wolff, we hope!"

Cocksure cackled in his success; except for Moggy who just raised his pint glass. Captain Jack Stupples did the same. The table went quiet. Jack would usually be outgoing and outrageous with his quips, his anecdotes and his tales of the sea. The trouble was that there were unanswered questions that troubled him.

Firstly, why had he kept on believing that he had spoken to a Green Fairy in various locations such as under the water and in his house.

Secondly, what was that thing that she kept saying? Oh yeah, the answer was inside him on how to kill Von Wolff. Jack was becoming slightly annoyed with the various riddles that he faced from her and his dealings with the obvious; Von Wolff. Granted, The Green Fairy was trying to be helpful, but her story had a few holes in them. The thing was Moggy seemed to take the words out of his mouth as if he had thought the same thing. He observed something about the Captain that he wasn't his usual self.

Moggy asked him, "Captain, is it the Green Fairy?"

Jack looked at him in shock and instantly came back with, "How do you know about that?"

"You told us remember," Moggy replied. "On the way back from Guernsey the other week. You mentioned that you had a dream about her."

Jack paused.

"It's true," Arkwright said. "We all heard it even though we were hung over on the New Moss Rose that morning."

"Oh yes," said Stupples. "But that was just a dream. I wasn't implying that it was real."

"Yes, I know," said Moggy. "But at the time you were hell bent that it was real, and then there was that time when you just seemed to freeze in your living room when we were looking at your map."

Jack paused again.

"It's true, Cuz," said Cocksure. "Are you okay?"

"Oh and also," Moggy said. "You said that you were pulled down by a current in the Med and then that Sperm whale pulled you back up again. But the tide doesn't pull down, it goes sideways, so how did you end up sinking that fast?"

Jack paused again.

'Well Moggs is not stupid,' Jack thought.

The crew looked at Jack while he paused.

"We are concerned, Cuz," said Cocksure.

'Any other story wouldn't work,' Jack thought so he told them the truth, or what he had seen and had heard, but he would leave one part out; that the answer was inside him and that there was a way to kill Von Wolff.

"Okay," he said, "for the past week and a half or so, I have been stalked by a Green Fairy who keeps showing up wherever I am and who keeps saving me! There you go I said it!"

The crew looked at him and blinked. Then a burst of laughter came from the crew members. Moggy seemed to relax.

"It's okay," said Cocksure to Arkwright and Mills. "He's all right, just getting a bit old, we think." He laughed again.

"What it is...," said Moggy. "Is that nothing has changed. He still pulls things out of the hat, no matter what the odds are, but as Cocksure said, he's getting old, a bit slower then he used to be too." Moggy laughed along with the crew. "But don't worry Cap," Moggy said. "We still love you. And as for the tide pulling you down in the Med, well these freaky things do happen." At that he laughed again and added, "We're just happy that you're alive and that you are still the same old you." He then patted the Captain on the shoulder.

"Yes, that's it," Jack replied, "just getting old." He then laughed.

It was a total lie, of course, because he knew that no one would believe him, if he told them the truth. Von Wolff and the advice from The Green Fairy was his problem and his problem alone, it seemed.

Jack went back home that evening to his wife Maud in the plains of Waterloo Street, where a bit of good news happened for a change.

"Jack! Jack!" Maud cried from the kitchen, as he knocked and came in. "Some good news," she said.

"What Love?" Jack shouted while taking off his shoes, his jacket and hanging up his hat.

"Well," Maud said, "a telegram came through on the machine. There is a new Absinthe contact for you to deal with and it's near, nearer then Brides Le Bains. This contact is still in France, but Brittany this time!"

"You're joking!" Jack said, and he ran through to the kitchen.

"No," Maud said. "This is good news, that piece of trash Lenoir put us in contact with him."

"Yes, it is good news," Jack said. "Yes, good news indeed."

The next morning, in his usual fashion, Jack strolled down to the harbour to meet Moggy at the repaired and now Absinthe less New Moss Rose. Moggy was there at half past six as usual, pottering around the boat.

"Mogg!" said Jack enthusiastically as he approached the boat.

Moggy looked up. "Morning Captain," said Moggy. "Have a good night after celebrating?"

"Yes, good Mogg," said Jack. "But never mind that. We have a closer contact to get Absinthe from, and it's Brittany this time. Lenoir put us in contact with him and we are heading there tomorrow. We're going to make a killing again Mogg, a killing!" Moggy paused for a minute and then the realism dawned on him.

"More Absinthe. Brittany, which isn't far away, more cash!" At that, he cheered and jumped up and down on the deck and he and Captain Stupples shook hands and patted one another on the back.

Captain Stupples said, "Right Mogg, with regards to the New Moss Rose, let's check that old steam powered Merlin engine of hers, shall we?"

"Right Captain," Moggy replied.

They both leaped down into the hull of the boat and went down into the engine room and opened the door to see the engine.

"Right, start her up Mogg," Jack said.

Moggy flicked the switch. The steam engine started to belt away with its metallic clanking. It ran smoothly until suddenly it just stopped as if it had died. Jack and Moggy looked at it, pausing for a minute.

Jack laughed quickly in denial. "Try it again," he said.

Moggy flicked the switch again and it fired up, clanking away.

"Excellent!" Jack said. Steam emanated from the exhaust on top of the boat until it stopped again with a clank. "Damn!" Jack said.

Moggy flicked the switch. This time there was nothing.

"What the hell," Moggy said. "The engine's knackered!" Jack bit his finger in anger. "Oh, I know," Moggy said. "It's the safety cut out on the heat exchanger. That part went last year! What happens Captain, is it springs a leak and the steam knocks the..."

"I don't care what part it is," Jack said. "All I know is that we need to fix it, because we've got to do a journey with it tomorrow!"

Moggy went silent. The trouble was that it was the same engine that powered the propellers on the boat, so they were 'stuffed,' as they couldn't just fly all the way there.

Captain Jack sighed and held his head down.

"Right," he said. "We'll just have to postpone our trip to Brittany for a few days and get a new part for the engine."

"That's fine. Right Captain," Moggy said.

"Well," Stupples said. "All we need to do is take a trip to Ted the mechanic and he'll fix it for us; simple really."

They both left the New Moss Rose and made their way as quickly as possible to the mechanic's workshop, in the centre of Ramsgate.

Ted, the mechanic who lay on the workshop floor, covered in dirt, fixing what looked to be a fireman's jet pack, laughed.

"Ha, the primary heat exchanger on the New Moss Rose. That is a Merlin steam engine," he said. "So to get a part like that won't be quick to get or cheap either!"

Ted was a fat little northern man from York with a beer gut and goggle eyes and he was drugged silly half of the time on Absinthe as well.

'What better choice for a mechanic,' Stupples thought.

Jack rolled his eyes. "Yes, yes," he said. "The price isn't a problem. How long will it take to get it fixed?"

"Let's see," Ted replied. "It'll take a month to build and to supply."

"A month to build and to supply...!" Captain Jack responded. Moggy put his hand in front of Jacks mouth.

"Okay, thank you," Moggy said. "We'll think about it." With that they began to walk out.

"Wait," said Ted. "To be helpful, you could always go to one of the auction houses and bid for one, there's one in there weekly."

"Where?" Stupples responded.

"London of course," Ted replied.

Jack took a train to South London the next day and he found the auction house in good time. Old gentlemen came from far and wide to bid for items in the auction house. Jack sat wearing a suit like everyone else there. His hair was combed and he was given a number.

Auctions weren't really Jack's thing. He was more of a townie and a sailor rather than a city slicker. The trouble was though that Jack would have liked to have sent someone else there but who was there? He couldn't send his wife there for obvious reasons. Mills was too naive, and he had problems with his mother. Arkwright was an idiot and he had problems with his girlfriend. His cousin Cocksure was uncool and although he stood a better chance than the other two, he was likely to lose out in the auction and worse lose his temper with someone, and he had problems with his wife. His friend Billy Cat A.K.A Moggy dressed up as a cat in his day to day life, so how could he send him there with no one batting an eyelid.

No, the buck passed by default to Jack. Unfortunate not only for him, but also for the crew of the New Moss

Rose who for the time being, couldn't get the Absinthe from Brittany to make a financial killing.

Stupples milled around the gaggle of old gentlemen in the auction hall. As he walked past, he nodded to a few, he caught the tail end of a conversation. He wasn't sure but it sounded like someone had spoken with a German accent. The auction would eventually start, with all the old gentlemen milling round and talking about the war and other things and then sitting down at the announcement of its commencement.

The Merlin steam engine was the third item to be shown after the old gentlemen had bid for other things such as a vase and a tomb. Jack woke up, and his eyes lit up at the sight of the steam engine, the third item.

The auctioneer spoke. "And now we come to lot three," he said from the platform. "An almost new steam powered Merlin engine." Jack looked again in awe at the engine, the very machine that powered the New Moss Rose. It was big, it was shiny, it looked good, and overall, it was a thing of beauty. There it was, pushed onto the platform, on a trolley. "Can I start the bidding at ten pounds?" said the auctioneer. Jack immediately shoved his baton up.

'That's not too bad,' Jack thought. 'We'll still have plenty of money, after I've won the auction.'

"Very good," said the auctioneer and gestured to Jack. "How about twelve pounds?" the auctioneer continued. Another hand popped up near the front. Jack just saw the back of his head. It looked somewhat familiar though. Then he heard.

"Seventeen pounds," in a German accent.

Everyone in the auction house gasped, not just at the German accent but at the amount that he was bidding and that early. It was a lot of money for a second hand engine. After all, it was just an engine.

'No, it couldn't be!' Jack thought. 'Damn.'

It was Von Wolff; he knew it! The German man who was bidding at the front then turned around and looked at Jack. The devil reincarnated otherwise known as Von Wolff smirked at Jack. Stupples heart sank and within a split second he knew exactly what Von Wolff's game was. Somehow he had found out that the New Moss Rose needed a new engine and he was trying to take the Merlin steam engine away from Jack by outbidding him.

The only trouble was that although Jack knew that Von Wolff was stupid and that he'd be ridiculed out of the auction for being German in the time of war; nevertheless, if he succeeded, he would have won.

As if mirroring his thoughts, the auctioneer paused and said, "I'm sorry sir, that is a healthy bid but I'm afraid that I'm going to have to ask you to leave, for your accent is not what we call healthy here in England."

Jack glared at the back of Von Wolff's head and laughed, so that everyone could hear.

Von Wolff paused and then said, "I am Dutch, and I have the credentials to prove it!"

Jacks heart sank again. The trouble was Von Wolff was well connected and probably would have gotten away with his statement, but there was more action to come. He wasn't sure what though. At that moment, some more auctioneers walked cautiously towards Von Wolff who was seated at the front and he showed them what seemed to be his credentials. That seemed to satisfy them, they apologised and then they walked off. The auction then continued.

After some hesitation, the auctioneer said, "Right can we continue. Do I have a bid at twenty pounds?"

Jack gritted his teeth in anger. 'Damn!' he thought. 'He must have some fake credentials!'

And, as if Von Wolff knew what he was thinking he turned around and he smiled at Jack from the front row. Jack gestured obscenely at him.

"Excuse me," said the auctioneer, who had spotted Jack's obscene gesticulating. "Can we be gentlemen in here, please"!

Von Wolff then turned around. The other problem was that, Von Wolff obviously, being in charge of a private army was richer than Stupples, so he could probably outbid him. Jack, however, ignored that possibility, and raised his baton at the twenty pounds. The crowd of gentlemen in the auction house gasped at the price that he was bidding for a second hand engine. It wasn't so much that Jack didn't have the money, it just seemed a lot of money.

Von Wolff responded, raised his baton again and said, "Twenty-five pounds."

The crowd in the auction house gasped even more. Jacks mouth dropped open. Something told him that he was not going to leave with the engine.

Jack gritted his teeth and shouted, "Twenty-nine pounds!" Gasps erupted again.

Von Wolff instantly replied, "Thirty pounds!" More gasps erupted, and one bloke fainted in his seat towards the front.

Von Wolff was paying a heavy price for a second-hand engine, and the other gentlemen in the auction house were thinking what was wrong with them. It was just a second-hand engine. But Jack knew Von Wolff's game. He wanted to make it as hard as possible for the New Moss Rose to smuggle the Absinthe from France into England by taking the only thing that could get the boat to France to get the Absinthe. That was it. Stupples just simply didn't have the money to bid higher.

The auction ended quite quickly after that with the auctioneer going, "Sold! To the gentleman from Holland!"

Jack sat there silently, gutted!

After the auction had finished Von Wolff walked up to Jack. The Merlin steam engine sat at the front of the auction hall, ready to be collected.

"Good afternoon Stupples," he said. Jack said something obscene to him and Von Wolff laughed. "Tough luck Stupples," he said. "Good luck ferrying Absinthe from France now!"

Jack looked up.

"How did you get out of the Mediterranean Von Wolff you piece of crap?" he asked. "As far as I could see, lightning bolts had trashed your submarine when we left you on that forsaken sea, and still, you arrive here two weeks later!"

"Ah well," said Von Wolff. "It is an interesting story. You see, my crew and I spent two days afloat at sea on that wrecked submarine. But you see Stupples; that is where German mechanics are better than English ones. I had a good mechanic on board fortunately, and we managed to fix the submarine and slowly but surely we sailed back to the south of France where my Zeppelins waited for me and then took me back to Germany. So, two weeks later, I could travel here to outbid you in the auction for the Merlin steam engine for the New Moss Rose. Which is the point!" He added and at that laughed again at his success.

"But how did you know that I'd be here at the auction today?" he asked.

"Ah well," said Von Wolff. "I have my contacts and my spies. Didn't you find it funny how the New Moss Rose's engine suddenly stopped working? Well, that was one of my saboteurs. Didn't you notice some German looking people, standing around on the day when you were selling Absinthe in Ramsgate's harbour?" He laughed again. Stragglers from the auction that had just taken place looked around at Jack and Von Wolff in confusion. Wolff saw this, he coughed discreetly. "Your world will burn, Stupples!" he said quietly.

Jack thought for a minute. The Green Fairy did say that there was a way to kill Von Wolff and that the answer was inside him, so he looked around for something to kill Von Wolff with. A chair, one of the antiques that was being bid for previously? No, that wouldn't do, besides that, technically speaking, Von Wolff was Dutch at the moment, so Jack would be arrested for manslaughter and plus he was a member of an allied nation. No, he'd keep his hands to himself and wait till Von Wolff was German again and then kill the 'git'.

The trouble was though that Stupples could sense that Von Wolff wanted to give him the engine, but that it would be offered in exchange for something else. You see in Von Wolff's mind, Jack and the New Moss Rose were going to be destroyed by him anyway at some point, by hook or by crook, so what Von Wolff was doing now was obtaining some leverage.

"Okay Von Wolff, what do you want in return for the engine?" Jack finally said with his head down.

"I thought that you would never ask," said Von Wolff quietly. "Well Stupples, here it is. I'll give you the engine if you assassinate the prime minister of England!" He barked with uproarious laughter.

Jack was half in shock at the idea, because this was Von Wolff who they were talking about, and this was one of the evil, hair brained schemes that he would come up with.

"If you're so well connected and so powerful," Stupples said. "Why don't you do it yourself with your private army?"

"Ah well Stupples," said Von Wolff, "that takes skill and months of planning. You are British and belong on British soil. You have a crack boat, the New Moss Rose and a crack team, with your friend who dresses like a cat. Why don't you do it? Besides, I need my army to plan an invasion of your coastline soon; Ramsgate, to be exact, on the twenty seventh of June. Plans are already underway."

Jack put his head down. He paused.

Otto Von Wolff thought that he had gotten the better of Jack, but he was wrong.

Jack said, "Thanks Von Wolff."

Wolff twitched. "Thank you?" he asked. "For what? I have just turned your world upside down."

"Yes, of course," Jack replied. "Thank you for telling me your plan. The thing is Von Wolff I also have my contacts, and I heard that you might also be here so I had to keep you talking to buy a bit more time until it became dark outside!" Von Wolff looked up at the skylight above the room, and indeed it was dark outside. Stupples carried on, "You see with all your cleverness and with all your power, you are still just an idiot, Von Wolff, because you forget one crucial thing!"

Von Wolff paused, and then he nervously asked, "What's that?"

"The New Moss Rose can still fly, you moron!" Jack said.

A faint humming sound could be heard that came from above the skylight above the auction house, from some sort of flying craft. Wolff looked up and then a spotlight shone down through the skylight, there was a crash and the glass from the skylight scattered all over the floor.

A man dropped down from above, dressed as a cat. Screams erupted in the auction house. He hit the floor along with the glass from the skylight, connected by means of ropes from above. The man hissed like a cat. It was Moggy but he had on extra thick brown face paint this time, making him look like a cat, to disguise his face.

More screams erupted. Von Wolff looked at Moggy in shock. Although he wore the face paint, Von Wolff knew who it was. Captain Jack Stupples then pulled a black balaclava from his pocket and yanked it over his own head. He pushed Von Wolff onto the floor while no one was looking, and then he ran towards the second rope that hung next to Moggy. Von Wolff fell onto the floor knocking into some chairs. Stupples then grabbed the rope and pulled it towards the platform at the front of the auction house and then he lassoed it round the steam powered Merlin engine.

At the same time, a second rope had spasmodically dropped down through the skylight with a loop in it. The New Moss Rose floated gracefully above the auction house as it wasn't being steered by the thrusters but instead by some makeshift propellers fixed to the back. Cocksure at the steering wheel, was barking commands to Arkwright and to Mills.

"Drop the rope you creeps!" he said.

Jack and the crew had spent the whole of the previous day attaching the steam powered, battery propellers to the back of the New Moss Rose and they were spasmodic in comparison with the thrusters. Down in the auction house, Jack pressed the button of a steam powered, radio buzzer that then signalled Cocksure at the wheel of the New Moss Rose..

"Right," Cocksure barked, "flick the switch!"

Arkwright flicked the switch of a big steam powered winch that Jack and the crew had put in place the previous day. Below in the auction house Moggy disconnected himself from the rope. He then stood back and Jack jumped out of the way as the massive engine was yanked across the auction hall floor by the New Moss Rose and it was hoisted up and out of the auction house through the skylight, and then hung below the New Moss Rose. Half the job was done, but the other half was to get Stupples and Moggy out.

Suddenly, Von Wolff jumped on top of Jack, grabbing him and pushing him onto the floor. The other gentlemen who had attended the auction stood back in fear. The trouble was the way that it looked, technically speaking, Von Wolff was just defending his property that he had paid for; the Merlin engine. On the other hand, Jack in his balaclava and suit, couldn't be identified.

At that point, someone had to intervene or to restrain the assailant; so the auction attendees came along and tried to grab Jack. Stupples pushed them off. Moggy pushed a few away from himself and Jack, and then he ran back to the rope that hung down through the skylight. He attached himself to it, and then another rope spasmodically came down from the New Moss Rose and through the sky light for Jack.

"Cap'n, we need to go!" Moggy said and then with the push of a button on his signal device, Moggy was hoisted up part of the way through the skylight, until he pressed the button to stop at the sight of Jack being grabbed by the attendants, on his way to his rope. Jack beat them off and they collapsed onto the floor.

Von Wolff was then back on him again. Moggy watched cheering for Jack. Jack eventually beat Von Wolff off by punching him in the face and knocking him back, and then he attached himself onto the rope or at least, got a foothold in the loop and was just about to give the signal to hoist him up, when Cocksure suddenly experienced some turbulence in the sky above. One of the propellers that propelled the New Moss Rose had stopped working, sending the aircraft spinning aimlessly around and around, while Moggy spun around underneath, and at the same time sending Jack flying back through the auction houses skylight below, still on the rope. He spun around at the end of the rope, catching the edge of the skylight, sending him crashing into one of the ancient artefacts in the auction hall.

The auctioneers and the gentlemen in the hall gasped in fright, then, to make matters worse, Jack crashed into another auction item, and then another one, spinning around, and connecting with all the items that people had bought. Von Wolff was then back on him, grabbing him by the legs, once the rope had stopped swinging.

"Let go you twit!" Jack said, wriggling his legs.

"No!" Von Wolff cried.

In the meantime, in the air above, Cocksure had left the controls of the New Moss Rose and he tried to get the propeller at the back of the boat to work again. He kicked it while the New Moss Rose spun around and around, powered by the one propeller. Below, Stupples had managed to get a leg loose and he then booted Von Wolff in the face with it. Von Wolff yelled and he fell onto the auction room floor. Cocksure above then noticed that a wire was loose on the battery of the propeller and he

reconnected it so that the New Moss Rose could be steadied in the air.

Moggy looked down and he saw Jack hanging parallel with the skylight, ready to be hoisted up. He cried-out, to the New Moss Rose's crew. "Hoist, hoist!"

Von Wolff jumped up and he grabbed hold of Stupples again, by his legs, just as he and Moggy were hoisted up together, by Arkwright who had flicked a switch. Just as Von Wolff went through the skylight, still holding onto Stupples legs, he let go because he didn't want to be pulled up to the New Moss Rose. He fell back through the skylight and he hit the floor of the auction room with a crash.

Von Wolff groaned and the New Moss Rose and the hanging Merlin steam engine flew away into the night over London with the thief duo Jack and Moggy hanging underneath. Von Wolff looked up through the skylight and groaned another one of Otto Von Wolff's plots had failed. Captain Jack had the new Merlin steam engine for the New Moss Rose which was the whole mission to London and Otto Von Wolff had paid for it; criminal really!

As for Stupples's contact who had let him know that Von Wolff would possibly be at the auction, was via Ted the mechanic. The moral of the story for Von Wolff was that tradesmen and mechanics do talk to one another and that was all that he needed to know as he lay on the floor of the auction room looking through the skylight in disappointment.

"Curse you Stupples!" he cried.

Of course, there was no proof that it was a mechanic though.

"Why fear Von Wolff, Stupples?" asked the Green Fairy who lay next to Stupples in his bed that night in his house.

"Well," Stupples replied who lay there underneath the covers. "He's powerful, influential and nasty. He's a bad man, and he'll kill me!"

The Green Fairy sighed. "Wolff isn't that bad," she said. "He's powerful yet he is weak. The only thing that is preventing you from killing him is yourself!"

"So, how do I kill and defeat him?" Stupples asked.

"Well," the Green Fairy said. "It's really easy Jack."

Jack's eyes lit up the answer he knew was finally coming.

"The answer is inside you Jack and only you!" she said and then she disappeared from his bed, in a green haze.

Jack woke up to discover that it was a dream and to find his wife Maud fast asleep next to him instead. He got up and he milled around the room for a minute. He looked out of the window onto The Plains of Waterloo Road and then he went back to bed, but he couldn't sleep for the rest of the night.

The next morning, Jack walked less jovially down to the harbour from The Plains of Waterloo Road to the New Moss Rose. He found his cousin Cocksure sitting on the deck of the New Moss Rose with an automatic rifle hidden underneath his jacket, he was guarding the boat.

"Morning Cuz," Stupples said to Cocksure. Cocksure with his eyes hooked on every nook and cranny of the New Moss Rose and on the harbour, responded.

"Morning Cuz," and then he yawned. "Is my two-hour shift over?" he asked.

Stupples paused. He said, "Yes Cuz, Yes, it is."

"I took over from Mills, two hours ago," Cocksure said.

"Yes, I know," Jack said.

Moggy took the first shift guarding the New Moss Rose when they had arrived back from London, for about four hours. He would have guarded it the whole night if need be. The trouble was that even though Moggy thought that he was a cat, he was still human, and he needed sleep, so after about four hours, and after a long day in London, he used Cocksure's steam powered communication device to call for someone else to do a shift. Next, it fell to Mills, who was then relieved by Cocksure after two hours.

The reason they were guarding the boat was because of Von Wolff's German spies and saboteurs sneaking about the place. You see, Jack had worked out that there couldn't have been many of them around, as it would have been hard for them to operate in England. Why did Jack leave useless people like Mills to guard the New Moss Rose, you might ask? Well, Jack figured that the spies and the saboteurs weren't going to be big German assassins, more like Wolff's own intelligence personnel, and there weren't many of those, so it'd only take one person at a time to guard the boat and it had worked that night.

Jack inspected the New Moss Rose. Nothing had been tampered with and the engine repairs were due to be completed that day by Ted the mechanic, so it would be watched all day by someone who was good.

Jack thought for a minute. "We can't carry on like this Cuz," he said. "Von Wolff needs to be killed!"

Cocksure put his head down.

"I have to do something Cuz," Jack said.

"What?" Cocksure asked.

"You will know when the time is right," Stupples replied.

Cocksure thought for a moment and then he said, "Oh I see... Wolff!"

"Yes," Stupples said. "But don't tell Moggy, he won't understand."

"Point taken," Cocksure said. "Good luck," he added.

"Thanks Cuz, thanks Cuz," Stupples said.

The whole of that day and the next was spent on the installation of the New Moss Rose's steam powered Merlin engine, by Ted the trusted mechanic, and at night it was guarded by the crew members of the New Moss Rose, each taking turns. Moggy started with the first shift, and Jack finished the last shift the next morning, with Cocksure, Arkwright and Mills in between, taking shifts.

Jacks next plan though was radical. On the third day after their arrival back from London, the New Moss Rose set sail for Brittany, France and with a hull full of hydrogen and guns full of ammunition. The crew were quite pleased to be getting another fix of Absinthe to sell and to make money on. The trip was quick, and it went well, and they met another 'frog' creep somewhere in Brittany.

Jack couldn't remember the name of the supplier. He paid the man and loaded the hull of the New Moss Rose full of Absinthe, before sailing back. A good trip in Jacks estimation; actually, a brilliant one!

'If only every trip to get Absinthe could be like this,' Jack thought. But alas something was going to stop them again.

Another trip was in order Jack thought in between their trips to Brittany in the next few days. You see, as a sailor there are many tall tales told at sea, many talks amongst sailors, many legends and many shipwrecks and where there are shipwrecks there is treasure; but what Jack had heard and had planned for was a treasure of another kind.

They left extra early the following week, after constantly manning shifts to guard the New Moss Rose over night to go to Brittany. They made money in the meantime though, with Absinthe coming out of their ears and selling it on the arm of Ramsgate harbour. They left extra early one morning to sail out just beyond the Dutch coastline to visit the wreck of a German submarine that contained something that was rather special indeed. Jack had heard on a day just before they had begun selling the previous batch of Absinthe from Brides Le Bains that there was a steam powered radar device in the wreck.

Yes, when Jack had told the tall yarn of the German steam powered radar to his customers, he wasn't lying. According to a reliable source, the wrecked sub had one radar unit and that it was the only one in the world. The sub had been wrecked by a British Q ship a few months previously. Rumour had it that there was a radar device on board and Jack loved the circumstances of it, for two reasons.

Firstly, it was a German sub in wartime and the sub was destroyed.

Secondly, it played to his advantage as the radar device was essential to his plan.

Moggy, wearing a diving suit jumped into the water just where the wreck was supposed to be off the Dutch coastline. Jack was at the wheel of the New Moss Rose and there was an air supply hose connecting the boat to Moggy. Moggy went inside the wrecked sub and salvaged the steam powered radar device from it. He came out of the sub with the device and he came back up to the surface with it in good time with the device attached to a rope. When it was put onto the deck of the New Moss Rose, straight away, Cocksure started to tinker with it, trying to get it to work by drying it out and stripping it down. He rebuilt it and it worked.

They picked up ships and subs left right and centre, all over the North Sea using the little screen that displayed little red dots on a circle as the sensor slowly spun round on top. Jack loved it. As finding Von Wolff in Germany was too risky, all he needed to do was to find Von Wolff in his little sub waiting to ambush him somewhere in the channel and kill him. The plan wasn't as straightforward as it sounded though. In every battle there was risk.

The date was the twenty seventh of June and the next morning Jack was quite sympathetic to his wife Maud. He kissed her and as usual, he made his way down to the harbour. He spoke with Moggy as he stood by himself at the dockside.

"Mogg," said Jack.

"Aye, aye Captain," Moggy said. "All fit to set sail."

'And to kill Von Wolff!' Jack thought.

Jack looked upset until he finally spoke to Moggy.

"Mogg," he said, "there comes a time when a sailor does not sail but stays at home."

Moggy didn't say anything, but he looked at Jack in disbelief. Finally he said, "What do you mean?"

"Just do as I say Mogg," Jack said. "You don't go on this journey my lad. There will be an invasion of England by Von Wolff's soldiers, here at this harbour today," he whispered. "Go to the Home Guard, lead them, tell them to fight. Tell them that I sent you, that will get them going! And above all else," he said, "defend my Maud, please!"

Moggy went silent and he looked upset. Finally, with his head down he said, "Well if it's got to be done Captain."

"Good lad Mogg!" Jack said, "Good lad, and thanks."

If Moggy knew what he meant he would have trashed the New Moss Rose to stop him and the crew from setting sail but unfortunately Mogg was naive.

It was seven a.m. and the New Moss Rose left Ramsgate harbour with Stupples, Cocksure, Arkwright and Mills aboard, with a hull full of guns and ammunition to go in search of Von Wolff in his boat or in his sub.

'More likely a sub,' Jack thought.

They spent hours, with the steam powered radar device ticking away, with Stupples staring grimly at the screen. The sea was calm that day, almost as if it was taking a deep breath before a plunge. Strangely enough, on that day there wasn't a single red dot in sight on the screen, not one, which was strange, and it was starting to become dark over the channel. They traced up and down the coast, sailing around until they started randomly weaving through the area.

The crew was silent the whole time, sailing in anticipation and in fear. Eventually at about six p.m. Jack asked, "Is the damn thing working?" referring to the radar device. The thing chugged away on the deck, steam emanating from the exhaust on top.

Cocksure came along, as he had had enough. "Well I think so Cuz," he said goggling at it.

"It's just that we haven't seen a damn thing all day!" Jack said.

Cocksure went silent and he looked at his cousin Stupples.

"You twit Cuz," Stupples said. "It's not working, you didn't fix it properly!"

He grabbed Cocksure round the neck who squealed as he fell backwards onto the deck. "Get off Cuz, get off!"

Arkwright and Mills had the sense to try and break it up. They were tired, the day was long, so an argument erupted between them all, until a beeping sound could be heard coming from the radar device. 'Beep! Beep! Beep!' it went.

Stupples and Cocksure looked at one another and then at the radar on the deck. Arkwright and Mills went silent. Jack leaped up and looked in the direction of the red dot on the screen which was towards the bow. It was Von Wolff he knew it and as there was no boat in sight, it was obviously a sub. At that a surge of water in the shape of a torpedo could be seen heading towards the New Moss Rose.

"Damn I've doomed us all!" Stupples cried out.

The torpedo surged on. Cocksure came along with a pistol at the bow, aimed at the torpedo in the water and shot at it. It blew up way before it hit the boat, sending water into the air. Jack shouted and he looked at Cocksure.

Cocksure looked at him. "Go for it, Cuz," he said. "Go for it!"

Jack nodded at him. "For the women we love!" he said.

"For the women we love!" Cocksure repeated.

"Men. Battle stations!" Jack yelled.

Arkwright and Mills grabbed their guns and Cocksure ran across the deck to the boat's controls. Jack continued to stand at the bow. Then a massive surge of water rose up in front of the New Moss Rose, followed by the top of a sub. A speaker climbed up from a hatch on top of the death whale.

"Good evening Stupples!" said a voice with a German accent, that Jack identified immediately as Von Wolff. "Prepare to meet your maker!" he cried as he laughed through the speaker.

Von Wolff in the meanwhile sat in the bowels of the sub with a microphone held to his mouth with an evil obsessed look in his eye looking through the periscope.

But Jack had a plan.

"Ted, fire!" Stupples cried out.

Wolff didn't believe his ears. He had guessed that Moggy would be back in Ramsgate with the Home Guard, but he didn't anticipate another crew member arriving on board the New Moss Rose at that moment. Of course, it needed five crew members to sail it. That was the whole character of the boat. Ted the mechanic popped up to man the decks machine gun on the New Moss Rose.

"Hey up!" he said.

"Oh damn!" Von Wolff said, through the speaker.

He had been tricked. Ted began firing at the sub at a rapid pace, laughing to himself as he did so. Bullets sparked on the metal half submerged body of the sub. For Von Wolff, it was time to submerge to avoid being knocked out in the first round. The sub slowly submerged bullets piercing it until it disappeared beneath the sea with a huge swell, but the radar had picked it up underneath the water. They saw the dot heading away quickly on the screen. Von Wolff meanwhile had no idea that they had the device.

Ted stopped firing.

"Oh," he said.

Cocksure immediately pushed the lever on the controls of the New Moss Rose sending the propellers spinning around. His eyes were fixed on the screen of the radar. The boat leapt forward in hot pursuit.

In the meantime, Moggy sat at the harbour, waiting and wondering.

'Did he believe the Captain, that there was going to be a German invasion that evening? After all, no one had come.' But then again, in Moggy's experience the Captain had a knack of being right, so he waited.

Moggy with all his good will, tried to tell the Home Guard Brigade that there was a tip-off that there might be an invasion by the Germans that day. Although they were sceptical and were talking to a man dressed as a cat, they believed him to a degree, as after all, it couldn't be that farfetched.

The trouble was that they had waited all day by the harbour and no one had come, so they went back to the depot and had thought that Moggy was mad. Suddenly, Moggy started to hiss at the sight of a mass of approaching boats that were obviously German, in the moonlight. He got up and he ran as fast as his legs would carry him back to the Home Guard Brigade's depot and crashed through the door.

"Get up you twits," he cried. "The Germans are here now, just off the coast!" The Home Guard were ignorantly all asleep in the depot. Moggy sighed and then he started to ring the doorbell as hard as his arm would allow him to get them all up. "The Germans are here; the Germans are here at the harbour!" he cried.

Captain Smith woke up on his sleeping mat on the floor.

"Aww Moggy shut up!" he said. "We all know that you're round the twist!"

"No, they're definitely here!" Moggy cried "At the harbour! Get up you fools!"

They all grumbled and shouted obscenities at Moggy. But Moggy wasn't that much of a fool.

"I'm Captain Jacks first mate," he said, "and I command you to get up and fight!"

Captain Smith opened his eyes and said, "Damn,, he's right! I forgot about that!" He jumped up as fast as his old legs would take him and cried. "To arms men, to arms!"

Moggy clenched his fist in success. He took up his rifle and started to run back towards the harbour. The Home Guard Brigade all jumped up, grabbed their rifles from the wall opposite and they followed Moggy to the harbour.

Meanwhile, back in the channel the New Moss Rose trailed the red dot on the screen of the radar device; which of course, was Von Wolff's sub. It trailed spasmodically underneath the water and the New Moss Rose followed above it, through the water. That was Jack's theory anyway; and this time, there was no fleeing, no turning back. No, Jack was prepared to see this one through.

Every now and again, they would just about manage to get above the sub in the water and drop a few depth charges, to try and destroy it, but it didn't seem to have any effect, as the red dot on the radar would just keep moving around on the screen. They followed it for a good half an hour before it suddenly popped up with a splash in the New Moss Rose's spot light to the right of them, somewhere off the coast of Portsmouth, to get more air.

It seemed that Jack had the better of Von Wolff though, as once again, Ted the mechanic opened fire on the sub from the deck-mounted machine gun. Bullets sparked against the side of the sub. The trouble for the sub was that while the sub was slowly turning around to face them so as to fire its torpedoes, it was slowly getting damaged.

"Cuz, drive straight at it!" Jack shouted to Cocksure.

"Okay!" Cocksure shouted and he turned the wheel right around and pushed the throttle forward, heading at full speed straight at the side of the sub.

Ted the mechanic continued to fire at the submarine. Otto Von Wolff was stupid, but he wasn't powerless. The sub also had an on-deck machine gun, but this one had a shield in front, whereas the New Moss Rose didn't, and it started to fire back. Bullets pierced the bow of the New Moss Rose. Ted dived away from the machine gun to get out of the way of the bullets.

"Turn to starboard to get out of the way!" Stupples shouted as he dived onto the deck to dodge the bullets.

Cocksure, crouching out of the way of the machine gun did as he was told, and turned the steering wheel to get the New Moss Rose out of the way. The bullets from the machine gun on the sub hit the side of the boat. Otto Von Wolff's sub faced them. Jack waited to be blown to pieces by a torpedo, but none came! He had his suspicions. He looked out the back of the New Moss Rose and he saw the speaking tube pop back up.

"Stupples..." in a condescending voice. "You can't win! I am more powerful then you!"

At that point, Jack and his crew felt a tug on the boat. The crew fell forwards onto the deck; the boat lurched and stopped and Jack looked back to find that there was a chain attached to the back of the New Moss Rose, that looped underneath, with a big hook which held the New Moss Rose. The sub had launched a missile and it was an insidious one. Von Wolff was playing with them.

"I could blow you to pieces if I wanted to Jack!" And then there was a mad laugh.

Jack used the opportunity. "Keep the New Moss Rose pulling!" he shouted to Cocksure.

Cocksure did as ordered, and then Jack jumped into the sea and pulled himself as fast as his arms could along the chain, over to the sub, armed with a pistol and a knife. Von Wolff in the meantime, was barking about his success through the speaker in the dark.

Jack reached the sub; this was it, the death of Von Wolff, he could sense it! He clambered up onto the sub, and snuck past the soldier who manned the machine gun; and who seemed to be firing at anything that moved on the New Moss Rose. Just then, Von Wolff popped up from the hatch with a loaded pistol pointed at Jack. Jack didn't have a pistol in his hand.

"Aha," Von Wolff said. "You fell for it Stupples!" Jack shocked stopped moving. "You see," Von Wolff continued, "I wasn't really playing games with you, I just wanted the pleasure of killing you personally! The New Moss Rose is going to be destroyed anyway. Ha!" Jack was taken a back. "You see Jack," he said. "You have your God, Absinthe, the Green Fairy, but my army and I have our God as well, the God of Schnapps!" He cackled madly as he took a swig out of a bottle of Schnapps that he had pulled out of his pocket. "Who will win Jack, who will win. Ha! ha!" Jack looked on in fear.

Then a duel erupted in time, matter and space. Or should I say The Duel. It was a duel between The Green Fairy and the God of Schnapps. Through the clouds and the sky above through the brilliant sunlight, the Green Fairy emerged with her green, razor sharp and powerful green wand, but she looked as if she was lost and she stumbled. Not long after, the God of Schnapps appeared with a duelling sword, walking through the clouds leisurely. He was tall and he wore green as well, with an army hat. The Green Fairy eyed him.

"Yes," said the God of Schnapps in a harsh voice. "Now you have come to your end, Green Fairy! Jack and his crew will not survive the attack from Von Wolff, and you will die!"

The Green Fairy looked at him and said, "Jack and his crew are a little foolhardy, but they are strong!"

The God of Schnapps looked at the Green Fairy in a challenging way and shouted, "Die!" He lunged towards her with his sword and she parried it.

Meanwhile, in Ramsgate, Moggy and the Home Guard Brigade had lined the harbour in tactical defence in any way that they could, from boats moored on the jetties and on the arm, to rifles pointed at the small boats heading towards the harbour, full of German soldiers.

"Hold steady!" Moggy cried. "On my command, fire!" he shouted.

The brilliant thing was that in the darkness, the German soldiers had no idea that they were there, waiting for them. They came close enough.

"Fire!" Moggy cried.

Bang, bang, bang, the rifles sounded around the harbour, and with good effect as the soldiers one by one flew out, left right and centre from the boats and into the water, killed by the precise shots. Moggy fired and reloaded and fired again, in hatred at the hundreds of soldiers coming into the harbour, defending his home and Jacks wife, Maud.

The soldier who had manned the deck-mounted machine gun appeared next to Stupples, an automatic rifle in his hand.

"You see," Von Wolff said, "this is what you call a no-win situation!" He laughed.

Just then a wave hit the side of the sub, causing Von Wolff to fall against the hatch. Jack seized the opportunity and within a split second he booted Von Wolff's hand as hard as he could, knocking the pistol out of his grasp and into the water. Von Wolff fell down the hatch. At the same time, the soldier with the automatic rifle fell towards Stupples and Jack grabbed the rifle off him, throwing him into the water, then he shot him. In the struggle, the hatch had closed and was sealed, and the sub started to submerge again. Jack let go of the gun and he was left afloat in the water after the submarine had submerged. Thankfully, because of the buoyancy of the New Moss Rose the chain that was attached to the boat released, and the sub sank, leaving Jack afloat in the water.

He engaged his radio powered beacon so that the New Moss Rose would come around to pick him up, and it did. Jack climbed out of the water and stumbled onto the deck of the New Moss Rose only to find Arkwright standing over him. He helped him up.

"What do we do now, Captain?" he said.

Ted the mechanic waited, perched on the deck gun. Cocksure at the boat controls kept the New Moss Rose turning around randomly, to avoid any torpedoes, keeping his eyes cocked on the water and on the radar screen.

"Arm the nets!" Jack said.

The duel between the Green Fairy and the God of Schnapps carried on in space and a storm erupted behind the villain of Schnapps as he fought the Green Fairy. 'Chink, chink', the wand and the sword went, as they parried and smashed away at one another. The Green Fairy turned her wand and she swung away as the God of Schnapps defended himself.

"Damn you Green Fairy and all the help that you gave Stupples!"

They parried again crossing a supernova in space in the process.

"You can't stop me!" said the Green Fairy. "No never!"

Moggy aimed his rifle at a German soldier in one of the boats and he fired at his helmet. The soldier fell down onto the boat with a cry. The sounds of many shots could be heard all around the harbour randomly echoing through the town. The Germans fired pot shots back at the arm from the boats coming into the harbour, but it had minimal effect as only a few of the Home Guard Brigade were hit. You could hear their screams now and again. Something about the light of the moon seemed to reveal the German soldiers in their boats more than Moggy and the Home Guard on the arm. Moggy continued to fire with precision, using the ammunition on his belt and the stash next to him on the harbour floor.

"Hold steady!" he cried over the sound of the guns to the Home Guard Brigade. Captain Smith complied.

Jack and the crew of the New Moss Rose cast huge nets over the side of the craft into the water, just where the radar showed the location of Von Wolff's sub. Mills, dilly dallied around and despite his bad hand-eye coordination he spasmodically threw parts of the net over the side of the boat. Ted helped to cast the net over the side.

"Why can't we inflate the Zeppelin on top?" Arkwright asked. "And shoot at Von Wolff's sub from above when it comes up for air or drop depth charges on it, or something?"

Jack studied the screen on the radar device and the blackness of the sea in the ships spotlight.

Granted it was the smartest thing Arkwright had ever come up with, but Jack simply said nothing. He had a feeling that they would need the Zeppelin on top as a last resort. After a few minutes of Arkwright keeping the sub busy circling around and around with depth charges, and dropping them, the net actually caught something, which was obviously the sub!

'Yes!' Jack thought.

You see it may sound silly trying to catch a submarine with a net, but it seemed to work. The problem was though that the New Moss Rose was too buoyant and the sub didn't have enough power to pull the ship underwater, so all they had to do was to wait for the sub to run out of oxygen as it was trapped below the surface and then kill

Von Wolff and his soldiers in the sub. Brutal you might think, but that is the sad thing about war.

The downside was that they had to wait half an hour for it to run out of air and the problem was that a lot could happen in half an hour. They couldn't lift the sub up with the Zeppelin on top of the Smack and destroy it that way either as it was too heavy, and the sub couldn't pull the ship underwater because of buoyancy, so they were in a stalemate at sea in the night. Jack worked out the odds. The crew constantly circulated around the boat, looking over the side for any German stragglers coming up from the sub so that they could shoot them and Stupples kept an eye open for Von Wolff.

'Who knows what they're planning in the sub below,' he thought.

"How dare you give Stupples advice on how to defeat Von Wolff and then send that Sperm whale to rescue him in the sea!" said the God of Schnapps, lunging forward with his sword at the Green Fairy, on a high mountain surrounded by thunder and lightning.

"I think that you'll find that I can do what I want!" she said and parried the sword with her wand.

The battle continued through time and space. The Green Fairy and the God of Schnapps were old enemies.

"Like the time when you approached him on his boat, the New Moss Rose," said the God of Schnapps. "You had no right!"

"Oh yes I did," said the Green Fairy. "You took my body remember!"

"Curse you Fairy!" cried the God of Schnapps and lunged forward with his blade.

The sheer numbers of German soldiers on Ramsgate harbour proved too much for the Home Guard. They were getting the better of Moggy and the Home Guard Brigade's fire power; meaning that the German boats were beginning to swamp the harbour. Bullets had hit somewhere on the arm near Moggy which meant they were getting close enough to see them. Moggy fired back. More of Von Wolff's private army were shot in their boats. It was very hard to see in the dark, but they do reckon that cat's have such good eyesight. Captain Smith lay against some sand bags on the arm, his rifle's sight fixed on the enemy. Germans and members of the Home Guard Brigade got shot and cried out during the night, amidst the crack of the guns.

Suddenly, after about twenty minutes, the radar started to beep and the red dot on the screen, which was Von Wolff's sub, started to move.

"Damn!" Stupples cried, "The net must have come loose! Pull it up to see!"

Arkwright, Mills and Ted the mechanic all hauled the net up while Jack eyed the radar screen. 'Beep, beep', it went. The net came up. There were rips in the rope. They must have cut through it somehow! They all looked on in disbelief. The radar dot moved, and Cocksure swung the spot light in its direction. A slight ebb of a mass of water then rippled towards the north in the sea, in the direction of the red dot on the radar screen. Ted, the mechanic aimed the machine gun at the ebb. The long white swell of a torpedo could be seen coming straight at them. Jack yelped and he fired at it with his automatic machine gun whilst yelling, "Port, port!" at Cocksure. Cocksure swung the steering wheel hard.

"And the time when you approached Stupples in his house," continued the God of Schnapps while the Green Fairy hopelessly stabbed at him with her wand with minimal effect, because the God of Schnapps kept parrying it. "Again no agreement!" he said.

They were fighting in a void of space now.

"I don't need one!" the Green Fairy said.

The Schnapps God paused and then he started hacking away again. The Green Fairy parried and spun around hitting his sword and then she punched him in the face. She then tried to stab him, but he hit her wand with his blade.

"Why do you try to do good, Fairy?" the God of Schnapps said. "What's in it for you?"

The Green Fairy swished her razor-sharp wand around but missed. The God of Schnapps dodged it.

"Courage!" the Green Fairy said as the God of Schnapps stabbed.

The crowd of German soldiers became thicker and thicker until the front ones reached the harbour arm while being shot at in the process. Grappling hooks were thrown up and the soldiers started to climb up. Some got shot, some reached the top and Moggy and the Home Guard Brigade's bullets were starting to run out rapidly.

Moggy shot at a soldier climbing up with his rifle, on a rope. He screamed and fell into the water below, dead.

Moggy levered the grappling hook off the arm with his rifle thus causing the rope to drop into the water with all the soldiers on it.

The fire power was concentrated on the gap where the two arms met in in middle of the harbour, with more of the Home Guard soldiers there, firing away.

"Hold fast!" Moggy cried. "The tighter we stay the stronger we are!"

The Home Guard soldiers who heard him did as he said, and as for the others, well they just did what the others did so it worked okay. At that point something tragic happened though; Captain Smith got shot.

"Ahh!" he cried, as a bullet hit him in the gut.

He dropped his rifle and fell back onto the harbour arm.

"Smith!" Moggy cried out, as he leaned down to help him. "Smith," he said, "are you okay?"

"No," Smith cried. "We're going to lose. We're out numbered!" Blood began to pour from him.

Moggy hung his head and looked on in silence. The Germans poured onto the harbour and onto the arm, cutting through the Home Guard Brigade's flank and some running into the town. Smith grabbed hold of Moggy's collar and he pulled him down.

"Moggy," he said. "Defend Captain Jacks wife! I'll hold them off as best I can!"

Moggy assessed the situation, then he gave Smith his rifle and the rest of the bullets for it was all he had.

"You're a good man Smith!" Moggy said.

"Thank you!" Smith said.

Moggy gripped his hand and then left him. He ran as fast as he could around the harbour and up the hill towards The Plains of Waterloo Street, armed with a pistol that he had kept from his last voyage on the New Moss Rose. Smith propped himself up on the sandbags, blood pouring from him, and he fired away.

Moggy's suspicions were right. A gang of German soldiers seemed to be heading that way as well, in the distance in front of him, up the hill. Moggy didn't have many bullets on him, so he had to make them count. He ran faster, to get closer to the enemy. He was right; the gang of soldiers turned left onto The Plains of Waterloo Street, seeming to know that Jack's wife Maud was there.

'A tip off from one of Von Wolff's spies no doubt', thought Moggy.

He continued to run, considering whether he should take the shot, but they were too far away, until they found the number Jack lived at, and started to break through the door. Moggy though had the element of surprise. They burst into Jack's house to find Maud cowering in the kitchen. She screamed. Moggy ran in from behind, and shot repeatedly. He jostled with one, killed another, paused, and then sat on the hall floor, exhausted and breathing heavily. He had succeeded. He had protected Jacks wife, Maud.

It was too late. A torpedo crashed straight into the side of the New Moss Rose. It exploded, blowing a wide hole in the corked hull, sending water into the air and also into the boat.

"Damn it!" Stupples cried.

Wolff yelled his success from his sub; but fortunately, Jack had one more plan. Cocksure and Arkwright looked in fear at Jack. Ted cowered on the floor of the deck in fear.

Mills came back up from the hull and said, "Captain, there is water coming into the boat!"

Jack didn't say anything. 'Land, land was the answer!' he thought.

"Go towards land Cuz, before we sink!" he cried to Cocksure, who pushed the lever forward and pointed the New Moss Rose north towards Portsmouth.

They all put their life jackets on. Jack knew exactly what to do. You see, at that time in the war the country was surrounded by mines and Jack's boat, being a minesweeper, knew exactly where they were. Jack also anticipated that Von Wolff's sub was hopefully low on, or out of torpedoes by then, and that this was their last tactic, so he had Cocksure shine the spot light on the sea in front, instead of behind them.

"When I say Cuz!" Jack cried.

Cocksure listened intently. Jack just hoped that he wasn't wrong and that they wouldn't be blown to bits or sunk before they reached the coast of Portsmouth. The problem was now. The New Moss Rose was a lot slower because of the incoming water caused by the torpedo, which allowed Von Wolff's slow sub to trail them more easily and it fired on them with its machine gun, splintering the New Moss Rose's wooden hull from behind. Cocksure ducked behind the wheel, at the back. The journey seemed to go on for ages. Jack saw the swell of torpedoes come either side of the bow just skimming past. If someone liked near misses it was Jack, but he had the Green Fairy on his side.

"You can't defeat me," said the God of Schnapps to the Green Fairy. "I will never be defeated!" They were fighting in the sky again. "Von Wolff will kill Jack and his crew," he continued, "and he will defeat him!"

The Green Fairy swiped, stopped, thought for a minute. She said, "You're right. You are undefeatable!"

The God of Schnapps stopped, aggressively. Within a split second, with her wand, the Green Fairy had turned herself into a human or God like bomb. The God of Schnapps looked at her in shock and he turned to run, but it was too late. She blew herself and the God of Schnapps to bits and out into the void of existence. Then the sky was empty.

Jack shouted precise directions to Cocksure from the bow, with uncanny skill, almost as if he knew exactly to the smallest degree, where the mine would be in the channel that he was leading Von Wolff's sub to. But then again, that was Captain Jack all over; precise. Von Wolff's sub was just behind them then, and getting dangerously close. The crew of the New Moss Rose remained on the deck of the boat, crouching to avoid the bullets of the sub's machine gun that was travelling along half submerged behind them. Jack flicked his hand to Cocksure to inflate the Zeppelin, Cocksure did as ordered. The Zeppelin on top of the Smack began to inflate.

The soldier who manned the machine gun shot at the cotton mass that was being inflated, but it was useless it just made holes in it. Two minutes later with a crazed look, Von Wolff's face appeared through the periscope.

Jack cried, "Thrusters!" and Von Wolff's face dropped.

The New Moss Rose leapt into the air, leaving Von Wolff's sub heading straight towards a mine that he hadn't seen in front of him.

"Damn!" he cried.

Otto Von Wolff's submarine hit the mine causing a massive, yellow explosion. The New Moss Rose flew up into the air, safe and out the way of it. The crew of the New Moss Rose cheered and leapt around in joyous dancing. Jack and Cocksure pumped hands on the deck. The sub exploded catching on fire, and the flames spread across the water. Von Wolff was sure to be dead inside the sub. The flames of the sub lit up the sea, but as the craft hovered above the fire, something happened. The New Moss Rose started to drop back down towards it, fast and they were headed for a burn.

"What the…" Stupples said, and looked up at the round, cotton Zeppelin on top. It had a rip in it, on one side. Hydrogen was escaping and they were losing height! "Damn!" Stupples cried. The crew gasped. Jack ran to the thrusters to engage them to miss the flames beneath, but they didn't work. "Damn!" Jack cried again and he ran down into the hull to find that the engine room had been flooded by the water. Jack came back up. "We're all dead!" he cried. "The engines are flooded!" Arkwright, Mills and Ted wet themselves in fear.

John Cocksure was first to attend to the rescue. "Leave it to me Cuz," he said. "Just get us to shore by assembling the makeshift propellers in the hull that are now submerged!"

Cocksure then grabbed a steam pipe wrench from the deck and a rope and he started climbing up the mast to the cotton mass which was the Zeppelin with the pipe wrench tied to his back. The New Moss Rose continued to lose altitude. The trouble was something happened then that smacked of pure evil. The boat suddenly jerked in the air, as if someone had cut one of the ropes connecting it to the Zeppelin and the whole ship tipped back a little bit. The crew of the New Moss Rose stumbled off the deck and over the back of the boat falling with a yell, but not Jack. He just managed to grab hold of the mast to stop himself from falling. He looked round and he gasped, thinking that his crew had fallen into the fire. But he saw the three of them Arkwright, Mills and Ted, hanging from the chain that was in the back of the New Moss Rose that had been connected to Von Wolff's sub.

Jack looked up to see Cocksure still hanging on the rope ladder above, near the cotton mass as well. The trouble was that Jack didn't know how long the trio could hold onto the chain, behind the boat and he couldn't pull them all up by himself. The boat continued to lose altitude. Cocksure reached the rip in the zeppelin by scaling the ropes around the side and he threaded the rope that was wrapped round him around the rip and then wound the pipe wrench round it with all his might, gritting his teeth. Around and around the pipe wrench went, forming a windlass to seal the rip. It worked. The New Moss Rose stopped dropping just above the burning sub!

Jack looked up and shouted, "Yes!"

If the devil had a nationality though, it would be German because just as the boat stopped falling, something hit Jack on the back of the head and he fell forward and stumbled around dizzily on the tilted deck, only to see the face of the devil next to him who had dropped down from a rope above.

"Good evening Stupples!" said the German who had just dropped down next to him on the tilted deck. Jack gasped and looked. It was Von Wolff! He must have grabbed one of the ropes above him when the sub exploded. "Yes," said Von Wolff with a crazed look in his eye, his glasses steamed up in fury. "Isn't this a turn up for the books! You see us devils always have a trick up our sleeves!" Then he said, "I ditched my sub at the last minute and I climbed out and jumped up to grab onto this piece of crap you call a boat, the New Moss Rose, just before you took off. The only thing that I didn't anticipate was I had thought that the blow that I gave you across the back of the head would kill you! You are stronger than you look!"

Jack was weapon less and he stumbled around dizzily, trying to get his wits about him to kill Von Wolff. The hanging trio on the chain screamed at the sound of Von Wolff's voice, as they had guessed what had happened. They held on for dear life on the New Moss Rose above the flames in the sea below. Jack couldn't speak because of the blow to the back of his head, so he held his fists up at Von Wolff as a last resort on the tilted deck. Cocksure looked down from the rip in fright at the situation that his cousin was in. There was nothing he could do though, because if he let go of the windlass, they would fall into the sea and burn! He tensed with the pipe wrench gritting his teeth, yelling with all his strength.

"Yes," said Von Wolff. "Now Stupples you will die!"

He swung his fist at Jack. Jack just about managed to block with his right fist and then he fought back with his left. But it was pathetic. The blow he received at the back of the head had weakened him and Von Wolff just moved out the way and it missed him.

Von Wolff laughed and said, "The mighty Captain Jack Stupples, dead at my hands!"

Jack's hand and eye coordination was terrible and the tilted deck didn't help. He tried to take another swing, but it was useless. Von Wolff just moved aside, and with no help at all the situation seemed hopeless. Wolff was just playing with him.

"You..." continued Wolff, "The New Moss Rose, your wife and your friend who dresses like a cat are all dead!"

Jack thought for a second, and managed to say in a weak voice, "Moggy is defending Ramsgate, England and my wife with the Home Guard Brigade and he will win!"

Von Wolff looked shocked and then he said, "Ha, if they defeat that wave of my army then that is just a part of it. I have more in Germany!" He smiled an intense smile at Jack. "The only way that they will stop is if my life beacon indicates that I'm dead," Wolff said. With that he lifted his jacket to reveal a machine that was strapped to him that would send a signal if he died. "And I am un-defeat-able!" he added and laughed.

Cocksure ground his teeth above, yelling, with the pipe wrench holding the boat together with all his strength, Arkwright, Mills and Ted hung off the back of the boat yelling. The situation seemed un-winnable.

Meanwhile, back in Ramsgate, Moggy the cat did what any loyal animal would do; he defended his friend's wife, Maud. She cowered in the kitchen at the sound of the approaching German soldiers coming down The Plains of Waterloo Road. They had swamped the town and Moggy and the Home Guard Brigade were defeated. Moggy crouched in the hallway with his pistol and a kitchen knife. If he was going to die, he'd do the right thing and not be captured at the hands of the Germans but die fighting. Members of the Home Guard Brigade were being taken prisoner in the harbour. England it seemed had been invaded and had lost the war.

Back in the channel Jack worked out the odds. Unfortunately, this was going to be the end for him but not in the way that you think. Jack worked out that he was heavier than, and even though weakened, he was stronger than Von Wolff, so that was his play. He lunged forward at Von Wolff just about grabbing him despite his bad coordination and locked him with his arms and his legs. Von Wolff looked shocked.

Jack looked back at Von Wolff and said, "For Maud!"

Von Wolff tried to move as he had worked out what Jack was going to do, but he was trapped. Then with all his strength, Jack threw himself as hard as he could to the right with Wolff in his grip, over the side of the boat and into the flames and water below of the submarine and they both died.

Cocksure screamed in agony at his pain and at the sight of his cousin falling. His job was done though. He couldn't hold the cotton mass together any longer, so he let go of the pipe wrench, it spun around, and it hit him in the face. At the same time a massive burst of hydrogen blew out at him from the open rip in the balloon and propelled him over the flames, past them and into the sea below. He passed out. Just before he did though, he engaged his lifesaving beacon. The New Moss Rose, still hanging in the air, was propelled by the burst of hydrogen above the cotton mass over the flames and into the sea below, landing safely next to the flames.

Hours later, Moggy crouched at the door in Jacks house in The Plains of Waterloo Street. A German soldier's shadow passed by the glass in the door. Moggy, with a hiss, instantly reacted by opening the door and then he drove the knife into the German soldier's chest who yelled and fell back and died.

A cry could be heard coming down the street. "Retreat, retreat, the master is dead!" with a German accent, obviously the commander.

'They must know that Von Wolff is dead,' Moggy thought, 'because his life beacon has signalled them!' Then he thought, 'Captain Jack has won, fantastic!'

The German soldiers in the street paused and then they started making their way back to the harbour to the boats. The English Home Guard soldiers were released and the Germans went back home.

Back in the Stupples house, Maud, Jacks wife said, "Thank you Billy, thank you!" and she hugged him.

Moggy left and Maud followed him, down to the harbour to make sure that the soldiers were actually going and they were; hundreds of them clambering back into the small boats to go out to the big ships out at sea. He and Maud then went to where he had left Captain Smith on the harbour arm to find him lying there stone cold dead. Moggy closed Smith's eyes as he lay on the quay, while the Germans left. Captain Smith had had his heyday in the 1880s but he was now dead and he was happy. He died happy knowing that he had performed his final service and protected his country.

"He was a good bloke," Moggy said disappointedly to Maud.

Maud put her hand on Moggy's shoulder to comfort him. Then they waited for the return of Captain Jack and the New Moss Rose. Maud waited for a while, but eventually she went home in shock. It wasn't long after the soldiers had left, that Moggy thankfully saw the battered New Moss Rose slowly enter Ramsgate harbour. It was still afloat even though it had a hole in it because of its corked hull.

Moggy leapt up happily and waited for the boat to moor. As it did though, the crew could be seen looking sad and unhappy as they looked at Moggy from the boat. Only Arkwright, Mills and Ted could be seen on the deck. They didn't say anything to Moggy, as they got off the boat carrying Cocksure who was on a make do stretcher. They put him on the harbour floor.

"Cocksure!" Moggy exclaimed sadly. "Is he dead?"

"No," said Arkwright "He passed out. We tracked him in the water with his life beacon."

Ted the mechanic said, "It's the Captain Moggy, that's the problem."

"Well, where is he?" asked Moggy. "He's not hiding in the hull is he and is about to surprise me with the news that he has killed Von Wolff?" He laughed nervously.

The trio paused in sadness. Ted the mechanic with a tragic look on his face then said, "No, he died in the flames Mogg." He took his hat off and hung his head sadly.

Moggy looked round. His head dropped and then he looked at the last light of the moon and he howled at it like a cat would, in grief. It was a sad night.

The next few days were spent silently mourning Jack. The crew met up every day and they talked things over in the pub. Moggy would just sit quietly, not accepting what had happened. On the forth evening Moggy sat at the kitchen table with Maud in her house.

"He went the way that he wanted to go Billy," she said. "That's good enough for me."

Moggy sat beside her, crying. They tried to comfort one another. Captain Jack's death was tragic in a lot of ways. A friend and a husband was gone, meaning that Maud would have to move back with her family to look after her.

Secondly, it would mean that the New Moss Rose didn't have a Captain anymore and thirdly, it meant that the crew would have to find work elsewhere in the factories or join the army in the trenches; including Moggy, worst of all, who had no known living relatives to help him.

Cocksure could use his engineering skills to build ships, but it wasn't the same as tinkering with the parts on the New Moss Rose with the Captain. But mainly, it was that a good man had gone. That was the tragedy. Many soldiers die in wars but the problem is the soldiers' relationships with the women who they love who are left destroyed at home. That was the deepest hole.

You see Jack and Maud used not to have many visitors because of their secret covert operations with the Absinthe that they had to keep secret. So, when Maud was alone, she used to look forward to Jack knocking on the door when he came back from smuggling Absinthe.

"I'll miss that knock every night from Jack, Billy!" she sobbed.

Moggy cried. A moment later there was a knock at the door. Maud looked up, surprised.